Midnight Treat

Other Ellora's Cave Anthologies

Available from Pocket Books

Midnight Treat

SALLY PAINTER

MARGARET L. CARTER

SHELLEY MUNRO

POCKET BOOKS

NEW YORK   LONDON   TORONTO   SYDNEY

Pocket Books
A Division of Simon & Schuster, Inc.
1230 Avenue of the Americas
New York, NY 10020

First Pocket Books trade paperback edition June 2008

POCKET and colophon are registered trademarks of
Simon & Schuster, Inc.

For information about special discounts for bulk purchases,
please contact Simon & Schuster Special Sales at 1-800-456-6798
or business@simonandschuster.com

Designed by Marie d'Augustine

Manufactured in the United States of America

10 9 8 7 6 5 4 3 2 1

Library of Congress Cataloging-in-Publication Data

Midnight treat / Sally Painter, Margaret L. Carter, Shelley Munro. —
1st Pocket Books trade pbk. ed.
    p. cm. — (Ellora's Cave anthologies)
1. Erotic stories, American. 2. Erotic stories, New Zealand. I. Painter, Sally. To kiss a gargoyle. II. Carter, Margaret L. (Margaret Louise), 1948– Tall, dark and deadly. III. Munro, Shelley. Curse of Brandon Lupinus.
PS648.E7M53 2008
813'.60803538—dc22   2007047663

ISBN-13: 978-1-4165-7723-2
ISBN-10:   1-4165-7723-8

Contents

✦

TO KISS A GARGOYLE
Sally Painter

TALL, DARK AND DEADLY
Margaret L. Carter

CURSE OF BRANDON LUPINUS
Shelley Munro

To Kiss

a Gargoyle

✦

SALLY PAINTER

Chapter One

can't wait until this afternoon, would you please check? . . . I'm on deadline . . . Marcy, Marcy Townsend," she spoke into the phone, while glancing out the window past the massive columns supporting the high exterior archway of her office window. Her stare shot past the delicate motif carved into the marble to his face. Leonardo! Her pulse quickened. The familiar statue jutting from the ledge was a magnet. She couldn't help it. She'd been enamored of the statue from the first time she entered her office three years ago. He rested on top of a huge pillar that rose from the 1920s building some six floors below the forty-fourth floor.

The half-man, half-lion gargoyle perched on the column, crouched as though ready to take flight any moment. His hard, muscled arms gradually changed to the legs of a lion with wide paws where human hands should be. His back legs were the same, transforming at the knees to those of a lion, complete with a lion's tail that arched and fell to the ground behind him. The legs supported a very powerful body. A human male body with wings retracted into a streamlined V shape along his back. His face, while that of a man, was clearly framed by a wild mane untamed and permanently frozen in the wind. His forehead was deep and furrowed very much like a lion's. But his body was sleek and hard, the torso of man. A very sexy man with firm indented buttocks tensed against the stance. Her longing for him pounded everywhere.

"If only you were real." She trembled, with breath rushing hot between her lips. If only she could touch him. The cold glass was smooth against her fingertips as she traced the outline of bulging muscles and indented buttocks. It was maddening. Obsessed! It was as though she were under some kind of spell. The need to touch him, stroke his sinewy, muscled body was so strong she'd even tried to lift the heavy window, only to find it was permanently painted shut.

"No package for a Marcy Townsend." The male voice crackled with static from the phone, ripping her away from the gargoyle would-be lover.

"Are you sure? It was supposed to arrive in this morning's mail. I'm on the forty-fourth floor, Marketing Department, Marcy Townsend."

"Yes, ma'am. I know who you are, Miss Townsend, I've been sorting your mail for almost three years now. I double-checked because I know it's urgent. You should check back after two for the afternoon delivery."

"Okay, Mister Jenkins. Thanks." She punched the button and tossed the phone onto the pile of papers on her desk. She still had time to make her deadline. The client said all final proofs had been overnighted to her, so the package would arrive in the afternoon mail. Clearly, she'd be pulling another all-nighter. She sighed and fell into the chair, staring about the room. Sometimes it felt as though she lived in the high-ceilinged, nineteenth century-style office.

She glanced out the window, letting her gaze travel over his sleek form. The all-too familiar impulses traveled down her spine to her pussy. Her libido was out of control. She longed for the sexy gargoyle to come to life and assume the role she'd fantasized him in—her passionate lover. His handsome face set her pulse pounding, sending urgent heat surging through her.

He was a powerful mixture, but mostly he was a man. A very strong man. A nervous quivering pulsed to her clit. While she loved this job, it left no time to meet a man, much less form a relationship. Besides, she pondered as she stared at the gargoyle, how could any man ever take Leonardo's place? Whoever had chiseled him out of marble certainly knew the male physique in its strongest form. Those muscles seemed to press against taut skin, conveying a sense of restrained power. If only he could come to life. Desire blazed through her at the thought. He'd seize her in those strong arms and make wild passionate love to her. All night! She jumped up and nervously paced in front of the window.

She'd created all kinds of scenarios of sexy encounters with him. . . . When night came, he'd transform into a man, take her in his arms and extend his powerful wings, flying her away to exotic places. There, they'd make love all night. Her sigh left a faint vapor on the window. Pressing her forehead against the glass, she splayed trembling fingers against the cool surface. Those fantasies of love had carved a longing in her heart so deep that she worried any real-life romance could never compete. Marcy forced herself away from the window, but her stare sought him once more. His male body seemed to shout for her touch, and she imagined her hands trailing over those broad shoulders, dipping over sleek muscles to glide along that powerful spine to firm buttocks. Fire lashed her throat. She would drink his kisses as his hands moved over her body, squeezing and stroking.

She groaned at the all too familiar impulses traveling to her groin and eyed the door to the private bathroom. She hated being a slave to her own pussy, but the urges were too strong to ignore. She stopped in front of the cold fireplace and glanced back at the gargoyle. Her heartbeat pounded harder with nervous anticipation. Heat throbbed between her legs as she hurried toward the bathroom. She needed him! The itchy ache centered in her clit, begging to be stroked. She entered the bathroom, thinking about her gargoyle, and slammed the door.

Leaning against it, her fantasy about the dark marble statue grew stronger as she lifted her skirt and slipped her hand inside her pantyhose. She imagined Leonardo, pulling her to him. Male fingers glided over her breasts and trailed in a scorching path past her navel to the heat and moisture between her legs. Her clit throbbed for his touch. She stroked, closing her eyes, imagining his large thick fingers rubbing harder and faster against the hardened nub.

"Leonardo." She kneaded the moist heat, quickening the strokes, faster and faster.

He'd spread her legs, lower his face to her pussy and slip his warm moist tongue between her silken lips. Her breathing quickened. He'd taste her, growl for more and in his heated need, turn her against the door, nibbling the tender mounds of her buttocks, slipping past them with his hard cock. The pulsing need writhed up her spine in a searing trail inching higher with each stroke. She could almost feel his thickness inside her. His lips nibbling her neck and his heated breath fanning against her ear were so real. Excitement burst to flame and exploded in shudders with the sudden molten release. Her body spasmed under the orgasm, her pussy throbbing against her fingertips.

Immediately, a bubble of sadness rose in her, threatening to erupt in a cascade of tears. She fought against the sorrow. She was insane to long for something so impossible. Leonardo wasn't real.

Her clit throbbed, reminding her of a man's cock when he came. The lazy orgasmic release clouded her thoughts. Absently, she twisted the faucet handle and leaned over the cold splashing water. She had to find a man. Not just any man—the right man. She plunged her hands under the rushing water. The coldness raced up her arms and the dying fire chilled under the sensation. Now she could focus on work. Lathering the soap between her hands, she held them underneath the water, but the pining for Leonardo pushed past the distraction. She pulled the towels from the dispenser and dried her hands. One thing for certain, she was darn lucky she had her own restroom.

"Marcy?" Her assistant's muffled voice invaded her imaginary world where Leonardo lived and breathed, waiting to please her, waiting to make love. Waiting— "Are you in the bathroom?"

"Out in a sec," Marcy called, trying to still the quivering in her voice. She flushed the toilet and turned on the water, inspected her shoulder-length auburn hair and checked her makeup for any signs of needed repair. Satisfied, she turned off the water and unlocked the door.

"I found the Madison envelope." The stout, older woman

waved the long Tyvek envelope in front of her. "Mailroom delivered it to Marcy Tooney over in Merchandising. Guess they can't read."

"Oh, thank God!" Marcy's legs wobbled under her. Trying to pull her thoughts out of the ensnaring sexual fog, she cleared her throat and reached for the envelope Nel held out to her.

"Are you all right?" Nel asked with blue eyes squinting in that maternal look Marcy hated.

"Sure." She snatched the envelope and sat down behind her desk. "Why do you ask?"

"You look a little flushed." Nel frowned.

"Just worried about this baby." Her hands trembled as she ripped open the envelope.

"How about an early lunch? I can order Chinese."

"I've got a twenty in my desk." She held the proofs in front of her, reaching for the magnifier.

"My treat. The usual?"

Marcy nodded, focusing on the proofs until Nel left. She dropped the magnifier and held her head in her hands, moaning over the reality that her fantasies had become all-consuming. This project was too important to neglect. Thank God for Nel. She was always such a lifesaver. She would do something special for the assistant at the end of the month, once the campaign was over.

The rest of the day was spent in meetings with her staff, going over the ad layout and pouring over the proofs until they were all in agreement with which shot to use. Even though she managed to get through the day, Marcy was constantly aware of *his* presence, drawing her attention away from conversations, distracting her so questions had to be repeated. By the time she was ready to concentrate on the copy, it was past nine o'clock and she'd missed dinner. Stretching in the chair, determined to allow herself a small break, her attention invariably gravitated to him. She walked over to the window and stood looking at him.

"I'm almost finished with the campaign, my handsome *leone*." She had no idea why she used the Italian name for lion, but liked the way it felt against her tongue when she spoke it. "Presentation will be in two days."

The need to nuzzle against his neck seized her. How many nights had she spent in long conversation about how much she wanted him and what she wanted him to do to her. It was absurd. She knew he was just a statue, yet every time she contemplated his muscled form, she wanted him—desperately.

Her stare traced the lines of his body she knew so well. She longed to trail her hands along the strong curves and knots of muscled arms. Instead, she traced them against the cold glass. If only he would unfold from the eternal pose and sweep her into his arms.

"You're my ultimate fantasy, Leonardo." Her heartbeat flip-flopped with the thought of such a powerful man making love to her. Greek legends were filled with strange half-man creatures and the gods who'd ruled over mortals. Had he existed during those times? She'd researched his origin and discovered he'd once perched atop a building in New York before being moved to Atlanta. Before that, he'd guarded a cathedral in Romania. She'd even made up a story about how he was once a man and had been turned into a gargoyle statue by the woman he'd rejected.

"I need to get out and find a living, breathing man." She pressed her forehead against the cool glass. It was bizarre to be so attracted to a statue, yet she didn't care anymore. It was frustrating not being able to touch him.

Each chiseled muscle and carved feather were etched in her memory. The familiar sensation tingled down her spine then raced hot and moist to her pussy. She stared at his face, straining to see his eyes, sensing he, too, wanted to be free and waited for her to somehow give him that freedom.

"Tell me how, Leonardo. What can I do to free you?" she sighed. "What is this power you have over me? Can it be real?" She shook her head, trying to separate herself from the burning desire coursing through her.

"Okay, Marcy. Enough of this," she murmured, trying to force herself back to the copy she needed to finish proofing, but the magnificent statue held her captive. She sucked in air, trying to still the overwhelming urge to break the window so she could at long last touch him. This must stop! Just last week she'd called maintenance and demanded they unstick the window so she could open it. They'd promised to look at it, but never showed.

If only they had. Her mouth dried. The thought of being able to touch him sent a rush of warm juices to her panties. To feel such boldness beneath her fingers would surely make her come. And just as she did every night, she gripped the ornate metal handles to try one more time to lift the tall window.

"Okay. Leonardo, if this doesn't open, I'm going to stop this crazy fantasy." All she needed was for it to open about two feet, just enough to reach through and stretch the short distance to his arm. Just one touch was all she wanted and then she'd be satisfied. She took a deep breath and gathered strength.

"One, two, three!" She pulled up, thrusting all her energy behind the attempt. The window didn't budge. She tried again. Nothing. Unshed tears knotted in her throat as she fought against the swelling disappointment.

"Oh Leonardo, I wish I could open this window and touch you." She collapsed against the glass. Within the realms of her fantasy, they were both trapped. The handsome gargoyle waited, needing her to touch him and awaken him from the spell holding him prisoner. Absently, her attention drifted up the long window to the lock.

Her pulse spiked. Who had locked it? It was never locked. Hope sparked deep inside her as she dragged a nearby chair to the window and kicked off her shoes. Her mind raced with possibilities. It had been unlocked since the first day she'd moved in, never bothering to lock it back once she discovered it wouldn't open. Perhaps the maintenance crew had fixed it after all. Hiking her skirt to her waist, she climbed onto the chair and stretched. She stepped onto the arm of the chair, then onto the back of the wingback chair, until it tilted against the window. Her fingertips brushed the lock. She maneuvered so she could grasp the metal latch, and twisted it open.

Electricity rippled through her. The window might actually open! Her heartbeat pounded harder. She looked down on Leonardo from the new position. She couldn't climb down from the chair fast enough, all the while reminding herself the window still might not open. Every nerve ending tingled alive. Her breathing quickened.

"Okay, Leonardo, I'm going to try again. If this doesn't work—well, I have to give you up—" The sob choked off the vow. She touched the tip of her tongue to her lower lip and slipped clammy fingers through the handles once more.

"One, two, three!" she cried out and pulled. The window scraped loudly against the casement and shifted under her grip.

Chapter Two

oo excited to move, Marcy stood trembling with the summer breeze blasting through the opening. The air rushed past her, fluttering over the papers on her desk. She bent down and peered through the opening. She was so close to finally touching him.

"H-Hello, Leonardo!" she called through the crack. "You're so gorgeous." She straightened and pulled against the window handles. This time it shifted to one side and refused to budge.

"I'm not discouraged easily, baby." The window groaned and grated against the wood. She squealed and pulled harder. The scraping echoed around her and then stopped. Tugging and pulling, Marcy realized it wouldn't open any farther. The tall window had stopped short of its length, giving her only a two-foot opening.

"I can still reach through this space." She stooped

down to examine the opening. Air tunneled through the wide space, shoving past her. The invading breeze raced around the office, lifting draperies aside, snatching loose papers from the desk and tossing them into the air. She eased her head through the opening, followed by her shoulders. The wind was cooler at this height and thrashed her hair against her face. She stretched forward, groping for his muscled arm. Magnetic pulses similar to the current of repelling magnets danced over her fingertips. What an odd sensation.

Her forefinger brushed a sharp jagged edge. The column base. She reached higher, but couldn't stretch enough to touch him. She'd misjudged the distance and needed to shift onto one hip to roll her body past the opening and onto the ledge with him. Slowly, she lifted her gaze to the gargoyle.

She kneeled beside him on the concrete ledge, surveying the inset and ledge's short expanse. She had done it! Her pantyhose snagged and ripped from the rough concrete. With her hair lashing in a chaotic, twirling mass against her face, she managed to capture the unruly strands and tuck them behind her ear. There he was! Leonardo. It was incredible! Her laughter was carried away on the wind. Her hands trembled. She must touch him.

Intoxicated by the victory, she slowly became aware of where she was—dangerously close to the edge of the narrow alcove. Timidly, she glanced at the busy street scene below. The city was loud and bright, and several hundred feet below—all backdropped by a full moon. The world spun around her. Panic momentarily replaced elation, but she looked away from the dizzying street scene and focused on Leonardo.

"Oh my! You're so magnificent," she gasped, looking at his sinewy form. His sleek, hard body was so expertly carved. Raw masculine power was captured in the frozen pounce, stopped just before he lunged forward into the air. She trembled as if he'd brushed his hand against her pussy.

Her breath latched in her throat, as she expected him to melt free of the stone and turn to her. Desire scorched a path over her, hardening her nipples in its jagged path to her clit. His face, only inches from hers, was the face of a man, yet his forehead was similar to a lion's with a long unruly mane permanently caught in the wind. How could a statue be so lifelike?

She reached out, but stopped short of touching his shoulder. To touch him meant the fantasy would end. When he didn't come to life, everything she'd hoped for would no longer be possible. It would all be over with one simple touch. Yet the temptation to touch him drew her closer. She drew a deep breath and steeled herself against the finality of the long-awaited touch.

"I've wanted you for so long, Leonardo." She ran her tongue over her lips. The wind swirled around her with the faint sound of night traffic ebbing below. She hungered for him. The need to feel him beneath her touch was stronger than any fear of losing him forever. Kneeling there, so close to the edge, she had only one thought. Leonardo.

She lifted onto her knees so she was eye level with his handsome face.

"Hello, sexy," she whispered, staring into his piercing look. For a brief instant, she wondered if he were in truth a wild animal instead of her sexy lover. Once set free, would he turn on her like a creature from the jungle, startled by human touch? Just inches from his face, she couldn't pull away. She was actually going to touch him. After all the nights of yearning for this moment, it had arrived. Her arousal released in a rush of hot moistness that drenched her panties.

Could she join him on the column without falling to her death? She didn't dare look down again. All she needed was to brush her pussy against his hardness. It was insane yet she didn't care. Some people had foot fetishes, well, hers was a statue. His name curled over her tongue and past her lips.

"Leonardo," she whispered, tracing the air in front of him in an outline of his bold face, still not allowing herself to touch him. Wave after wave of urgent need throbbed between her legs. Her nipples ached. She longed to feel his lips sucking the erect nubs. Fire streaked to her clit. His hard, strong muscles seemed to scream for her caress. She couldn't wait any longer.

"Leonardo," she sighed, finally letting her hand flatten against his face. The contact shot an electrical current down her arm, pounding her heart into a new beat. His beat. Lion and man, joined as one. Fierce. Full of raw desire. It seized her, leaving only a single thought in its wake. Leonardo.

"You're so gorgeous." She glided her hand over his jaw and down the length of his powerful neck to a hard shoulder. Her heart swelled with emotions. If only he could talk to her. She moved behind him, brushing against him so her nipples slightly grazed the cold marble. It felt natural to mold herself into his broad shoulders, flattening her torso onto his back, dipping between the V shape his wings formed. She longed to feel the magnificent body stand so she could enjoy him full-bodied. Trembling fingers curled around flexed arms bulging with steely muscles. He appeared ready to leap into the air with her riding his back. Any remnants of concern about her sanity fled with the feel of him beneath her. He was real. Her pulse quickened.

The marble was cool against her, but quickly warmed with the raging fire coursing through her. At long last she was touching her Leonardo. She glided up his back, tilting her pelvis so that her sex brushed against him. The contact of her hot flesh against the cool hardness of his back excited her beyond all fantasies. Frantic for more, she tugged on her skirt until only the thin netting of pantyhose shielded her from the unrelenting coldness of stone. She rubbed harder, riding the urgent wave of arousal with the friction stimulating the aching need between her legs.

Yet it still wasn't enough. She needed him to awaken. She had somehow actually expected it. Emboldened by the fire scorching her tender flesh, she glanced about the hidden alcove, making sure no one watched from nearby windows. Streaks of excited expectation shook her as she slipped the pantyhose and panties down her legs, and stepped from them. Cool air snatched the skirt and blew against her, sending a rush of heated moistness against her thighs. She leaned into him. Hard. Cold.

The sensation tingled against her throbbing clit. A deep groan parted her lips and sailed over the whipping wind. She moaned louder, with the wind tearing at her. Arching her back, she pressed harder into the statue. The contact provided the friction she needed. She was possessed and ground her hips into the statue. Still she was not close enough. She spread her legs apart, and dipped her hand to splay open the plump folds of her labia, separating just enough to expose the throbbing nub, and flattened against him again.

This time the contact struck her clit with the sensation she sought. Frenzied heat surged harder and she rode the waves of jagged pleasure until her flesh softened and melted against his stone body. She longed to feel him move beneath her and take her into his arms. Running her tongue over dry lips, she moistened them as she imagined his tongue entwining with hers.

Fire lashed hotter against her. Each wave of excitement tumbled over the last until a sharp electrical wave spiked and burst in a spasm of liquid fire. She flattened against his back, riding the final pleasures pulsing through her. At long last he was hers. Drawing her arms around his neck, she relaxed with a deep sigh. It was more erotic than any fantasy she'd imagined.

"You belong to me now, Leonardo." Her lips were a breath's space from his ear. "Did you feel me come? Do you know I'm touching you? You feel so wonderful. Do you know how much I've wanted you these past years?" Tears stung her eyes. "If only you were real, I'd take you home with me. Oh, Leonardo, I'd make love to you until you roared."

Absently, she wondered if she might be able to purchase the statue from the building owners. At least then she could have him whenever she desired. At that moment, she was living her fantasy, yet her heart felt as though it would break from the longing. She clamped her mouth against the sob.

"If only you were alive, my love. I need you so much!" Why hadn't he awakened? He was supposed to awaken and fly them to an isolated area where he'd make love to her—forever. Sadness gripped her and fresh tears streamed down her cheeks. She'd fallen in love with a statue, of all things. The silly fantasy she'd created was over.

She was possessed. She still wanted him. It felt so right! She belonged on the ledge with him. At that moment, had she been given the choice to become a gargoyle statue like him, she'd have said yes without hesitation. Eternity with her Leonardo would be a dream come true. Excitement slipped through her at the possibility of such a dream becoming a reality. A new fantasy to ride a little longer.

"Why can't you just *wake up*, Leonardo? I need you. I need you to be alive!" she sobbed, rubbing her cheek against his, longing to feel his flesh against her lips, to taste him. She pressed a kiss into his cheek.

Immediately, the stone warmed beneath her lips. She jerked from him, certain her sanity had fled. The statue began to melt from marble into flesh. How could this be? Surely she was hallucinating. His facial muscles twitched. His lips puckered. Then, his eyelids blinked and he turned his head toward her.

"Oh my God!" she cried out and stepped from him, realizing too late that she had shifted away from the ledge into empty space. The scream ripped from her. Frantic, she grabbed for him, anything, but all she met was air.

"Leonardo!" she screamed, tumbling backwards over the ledge. Panic squeezed another scream from her lungs as she plummeted toward the busy street several hundred feet below.

A prayer shivered past her lips. Scenes of her life and the longing for Leonardo flashed in front of her. Suddenly, steely arms wrapped around her and the sound of wings sliced the air. She looked up and Leonardo smiled down at her.

"Leonardo?" Her voice was strangled.

"I'm here, my love," he spoke and carried her back toward the ledge, only to sail straight up the full length of the highrise.

"Leonardo," she gasped and the world faded from her.

Chapter Three

arcy mouthed his name, but couldn't push any sound past the tightening in her throat. He stood in front of her. A virile, breathing male. No longer the half-man, half-lion statue. His forehead was smooth flesh as were his arms and legs. A man. A naked man! How was it possible? She cringed against the sudden reliving of plummeting toward the street. He'd saved her. She let her stare move over him. He was alive. He stood taller than she had ever imagined. Seven feet—at least. Muscular. Long, flowing, reddish-blond hair. Her brown-eyed gaze locked with his. Passion mirrored in that fiery stare with his human face set in deep furrows beneath his lionlike forehead. And he was naked.

"Oh my God!" she gasped.

"Marcy." The deep, rich voice melted her into a pool of desire. "You awakened me and nearly died as your reward.

I was worried I wouldn't get to you in time. I have waited for you for so long." He took a step toward her. The movement drew her attention to his hard cock, buoying under his strides.

"Oh my." Heat licked her pussy. He kneeled beside her. Strong fingers gripped her forearms, tugging her to him.

"It's me. Leonardo. I want to please you. Show my gratitude for awaking me. You have told me of your desires and wishes. I want to fulfill each and every one of them, now." His Italian accent sent a new wave of erotic pulses coursing through her.

"This isn't happening. I've finally suffered a breakdown from my crazy fantasizing."

His laughter sailed into the air.

"This is just my imagination," she insisted. "Or perhaps I fell asleep on the couch again."

She met his gaze, shocked to see not the half-man, half-lion, but the face of a man. Her pulse throbbed. A very handsome man with a broad forehead, squared jaw and strong chin, but it was his almost bronze-like eyes that held her captive, pulling each breath from her. She now knew where the stone tiger-eye got its descriptive name. Heated puffs expelled between her quivering lips.

"If I'm imagination, then you can wish me to disappear." His sexy baritone voice teased her. Could it truly be her Leonardo had really come to life? And saved her from a deathly fall?

The magnificent man stood before her, no longer the dark marble statue of her obsession. She longed to run her hands over his flesh and feel his muscles tense under her touch. Her stare traced the line of hair leading from his navel to his groin. Her pulse throbbed. His cock was stiff and erect in front of him and it was a very big cock. Oh yes, he was real.

"W-What happened to your wings, your mane?" she asked, dragging her attention to his face, needing to verify he no longer resembled a half-man, half-lion. His jaw was set in a determined clench, but it was the gleam in his eyes that assured her further discussion was not going to happen.

"My Marcy, I've waited so long for you to free me so I could be with you. I've burned with the need to make love to you. I've listened to your soft voice and yet was unable to tell you how I felt." He placed his finger over her trembling lips. "Shh. There shall be plenty of time to talk, later."

Heat burst inside her and raced in flashing pulses to her pussy. She slipped her tongue between her lips to taste his finger. Salty, yet warm, not at all cold as he had been only moments earlier. He was alive. A mere kiss had transformed him into a man—a very well-endowed man!

"Leonardo," she breathed. She longed to claim her prize, and reached out for him. Her fingertips met hard, smooth flesh. She trembled, letting her hand glide over his shoulders. Firm muscles flinched under her touch. His skin warmed with sweat beading along his neck as she let her fingers probe down his sinewy back, his skin growing hotter under her touch. "Can it be? Are you real?"

"I am." He wrapped his arms around her. Her breasts crushed against his powerful chest, warming against his heat as his steely body embraced her. Just like her fantasies, only better. Oh, so much better! She glided her hands over his back, luxuriating in the feel of smooth muscled skin rippling beneath her fingertips. Her flesh against his flesh. She stood on tiptoe to catch his kiss. The contact of his lips against hers sealed the bond at long last.

A deep groan vibrated from his chest as his lips possessed

hers. Warm, strong, they demanded more. A small moan slipped from her in a heated rush as she drank his kisses. He tasted so good, like hot fudge melting over ice cream. Her arms tightened around his powerful neck, as she longed to lose herself completely in his possession. Her mind swirled with the sensation of his tongue, flicking against her lips. She opened her mouth and lashed her tongue around his. Leonardo was alive—kissing her!

His scent of earth on a warm summer night filled her nostrils. She wanted more. She wanted all of him.

Strong male fingers threaded through her hair, then closed to tug her head backwards to better receive the kiss. His throaty groan was followed by tensing muscles as he plunged his tongue deeper into her mouth, sending her heartbeat into an erratic pounding. He tasted better than she'd imagined. The wild fervor twisted and curled through her.

If this was one of her fantasies and she'd managed to cross the thin line separating reality and insanity, then she was never going back. She tottered between ecstasy and self-doubt. No amount of fantasizing could be this powerful.

His fingertips trailed down her back and cupped her buttocks, crushing the skirt material in his firm grip. He pushed her firmly against his cock. Heated breath rushed from his nostrils, fanning over her face. His chest heaved. She moved her hand and pressed against his chest and his pounding heartbeat quickened. She slipped her arms around his back, trailing fingertips up and down his spine.

He responded by tightening his arms around her. His grunts muffled against her lips. Tightening her arms around his neck, Marcy arched against him. She longed to feel each tantalizing sensation of his cock against her wet pussy.

Images of that hard cock slipping in and out of her pussy sent hot, achy strokes to her clit. There was no getting enough of him. Taut muscles flinched under her touch, driving her frantic excitement to the very edge of control.

She pulled from his kiss, gasping. Her breasts crushed against his chest, she sucked in air.

"I want you, Marcy." He held her chin between his fingers and drew her back to his lips once more. His possession was fierce. His tongue thrust inside her mouth and reclaimed her tongue.

She slid her hand to his trim waist, gliding down to his smooth, firm ass. Sleek, slightly indented buttocks were pliable beneath her massaging hands. Her pulse spiked and once more a deep throaty groan vibrated from her and lodged between their kiss. She ground into his stiff cock pressed against her abdomen. Frantic to feel his heat against hers, she stood on tiptoe trying to make contact against her clit.

Suddenly, he broke from the kiss and scattered hot passionate kisses down the column of her neck. Strong hands molded around her buttocks, a finger slipping down the crease to tease her anus with firm circular strokes. She burned to be free of her clothing and tugged against the silk blouse.

Large hands assisted. The world faded into the darkness of late night, leaving only the two of them bathed in moonlight. Hot and trembling with the urgent need to feel him inside her, Marcy slipped the skirt from her waist, letting it fall to her feet. His forefinger glided over her hips and around to her abdomen, slipping between the lips of her pussy.

Her breath was a sharp intake, drawing her breasts higher. She waited, anxious to feel the pressure of his touch to soothe

the aching throb. Oh, how she needed it, just enough to give her some relief from the pent-up energy burning there.

He pulled from her lips, panting. Looking down at her, his gaze slipped over rosy, peaked breasts. He bowed to capture a bud between his lips and sucked, gently nibbling.

Marcy groaned. Fiery streaks shot to her clit and her hips undulated in a desperate attempt to touch his finger, but he moved it once more just beyond contact. He allowed his stare to slip over her abdomen to her pussy. A frustrated moan rushed from her. Smiling, he pressed his finger to the edge of her shaven pussy and stroked slowly, deliberately. He teased the lips of her pussy, dipping his finger between them, but careful not to brush against the tender flesh erect with desire and longing.

"Leonardo," she moaned, breathless and trembling with anticipation. "Please."

He inserted his finger inside the hot moist slit once more, yet paused. A disappointed groan escaped her.

"Will you please touch me?" she begged, but still he didn't accommodate the request.

She opened her eyes to the dark naked passion mirrored in his. Fine male lips slid into a wicked grin and he thrust his finger into her flesh. The sensation of his finger against her clit melted into a liquid heat that rushed hot between her legs. She rubbed up and down against the pole his finger created. Then, just as quickly as he'd provided some relief, he took it away.

She cried out. Before she could complain, he kneeled in front of her. A deep appreciative groan parted his lips as he stroked the outer lips of her pussy. She warmed under his regard. Firm hands glided over her hips to her buttocks, clasping her cheeks between them, massaging and kneading. His moist tongue slid between her lips, and at long last his flesh stroked against her clit.

The relief was instant and she cried out, her voice echoing into the quiet night. She arched backwards, pressing her pussy against his tongue, grinding her hips to the rhythm of his flickering strokes. She gripped his head, fearful he would move from her and once more leave her quivering and needful.

The heat rose up her spine, undulating and retreating then rising again. She wanted more. She wanted him inside her. As though reading her mind, he pulled from her pussy.

"No!" she begged. "I was so close . . ."

"Shh." He cupped her face in his hand. "I shall not leave you wanting, my love." He scooped her up into powerful, determined arms, cradling the back of her head against his forearm. Supporting them with his legs braced apart, he lifted her and drew her slender legs around his waist. His cock, hard and hot, pressed against her opening. She moved and slipped her hand between them, closing her fingers around his cock. He was so big—how was she going to be able to take him inside her? Pushing her hand aside, he guided his cock into her opening. Every nerve ending tingled alive as he pressed himself into her. She was tight and tried to relax under his thickness, longing to have him fill her completely.

"I want you, Marcy," he groaned and pulled his cock from her, and then eased back in past the tightness of her opening. Gasping, with arms about his steely neck, she received his stiff, hot shaft. The never-ending emptiness was replaced with heated contentment. She moved slowly at first, and as she released her breath, relaxed around his thick cock, driving him deeper inside.

Her senses roared as his mouth possessed hers once more. The night pushed against them. He was driven beyond passion, beyond desire. He was like an animal, pumping his cock into her, holding her by the hips, pulling her up his shaft and then down again as he ground himself into her. Heated strokes raced up her spine with each thrust of his thick cock. Sweat beaded over his bulging muscles and he shifted, balancing as he leaned forward. Her nostrils filled with sweat and man. She clung to him, gripping his hard back.

The sound was new, but she immediately knew it was his wings releasing from the hidden slits along his back. He must have the ability to seal them inside somehow because now they were spread wide, blotting out the starry night. He lifted his head and leaned back, releasing a bellowing roar. Excited pulses skittered down her spine, heightening her arousal. Knowing it was she who had pushed him to the edge of need sent a wave of molten heat charging from her pussy, drenching his cock.

Tightening her arms around his neck, Marcy gasped when he lifted from the rooftop, tilting her back farther. His wings fanned down then up again. Leonardo positioned himself over her, supporting her in the cradle of his arms as he pounded his cock into her. His breath was sharp and fast.

He drove his cock deeper, all the while his wings supporting them. The sound of his cock slipping in and out of her, his balls slapping against her as he quickened his thrusts, set her pulse pounding harder. He leaned over her, with lips settling against her ear. Hot rapid flicks of his tongue sent warm tingles cascading over her.

"I've wanted you for so long, Marcy," he whispered, hot ragged huffs fanning her ear.

His voice droned in her mind, curling down into the haze of passion. He was real. He was here, fucking her in midair. It was better than any of her fantasies. Oh, so much better. Grinding her hips into his thrusts, she cried out. Excited streaks flashed up her spine. Waves of pleasure pulsed with each thrust. She tottered on the edge of climax and he arched from her, expanding his wings wider, and released a fierce roar into the night as he spasmed and went rigid. His wings stopped in mid-motion and they began to descend toward the roof. He lunged forward and pulled her into a final thrust.

Once more his wings drew downward then up, and they ascended above the building. Searing kisses claimed her mouth. She met the thrust, brushing her clit against him. She moaned and ground into him. The liquid heat of his seed filled her. He groaned, slowly grinding his cock into her, feeling as though she melted into him.

"Leonardo!" she cried out. Spasms gripped and twisted her. Sweet release throbbed and ebbed.

He straightened. Gingerly, he pulled his cock from her, so her body slid down the full length of his, then he set them down on the roof.

She molded against his powerful body, her pussy still throbbing. She wrapped her fingers around his hot, pulsating cock and stroked him, delighting in each throb in reaction to her movement.

A screech pierced through the night, jolting them from the contented release of their passion. It sounded behind them once more and Marcy jerked around just as the female silhouette bounded from the stairwell doorway.

"What is—"

"No!" the banshee screamed with dark hair streaking

around her face, captured in the lashing wind. "You cannot have him, spellbreaker!"

The world spun around her. Before she could cry out at the terrifying image racing toward them, Leonardo lifted her from the rooftop once more, this time rising higher and faster.

"Come back! You bastard. You're mine! I shall find you and turn you back to stone!" The voice echoed up to them as he flapped broad wings, carrying them away from the building and away from the city.

Her open blouse fluttered about her as he soared higher toward the canopy of stars, tightening his arms around her. His heartbeat pounded in her ear. Once more she was reminded he was a living man. Not a beast. Not a statue. A real man.

"W-What was that?" she asked, trying to catch her breath, peering over his shoulder at the twinkling lights below. She tightened her arms around his neck. "Where are you taking me?"

"Someplace safe."

"W-What—who was that?"

"A witch."

"Then I was right? You *were* placed under a spell?"

He looked down at her and nodded.

"How did she find you so quickly?"

"She's a witch, my love. But she won't be bothering us again."

"How can you be sure?"

"We'll go where she can't find us. At least, for tonight. A quiet place where I can make love to you."

"But why did she do this to you?"

"I was once a man. Four hundred years ago. Until I refused to marry a princess."

"And she turned you into a gargoyle? Like Sleeping Beauty. I can't believe all this is happening." She felt lightheaded and rested against his chest. "What's your real name?"

"Leonardo." He kissed her temple and brushed a strand of hair from her forehead.

"I'm serious."

"So am I. You're safe with me. Don't let her intrusion spoil our first night together."

"What's her name?"

"She no longer has one. To speak it would draw her to us. It's part of her spell. We will be safe. Trust me." He moved his wings and continued toward the distant mountain ridge. "I want our first night together to be perfect, Marcy."

His voice excited her. All worries about the witch subsided and she closed her eyes against the blasting wind and listened to his wings dividing the air. The rhythm of his flight was as exciting as any arousal. His breathing was deep. With each swoop of his powerful wings upward he took a long breath. With each downward motion he exhaled.

She rested her cheek against his bare chest, basking in the warmth of his flesh. Flesh! No longer marble. The thought sent streaks of fire to her clit. She needed to feel him inside her again. As if reading her thoughts, he stopped in midair and she peered around his muscled arm to the distant silhouette of a mountain.

"Asheville." He nodded to the lights along the distant ridge.

"How did you do that? Fly over two hundred miles so quickly?"

"I'm a gargoyle, my love. I can do many things mortal men can't and I intend to show you just what those things are."

She was mindless with only one need—to find the release only he could bring to her. He was hers. She had awakened him. And it was a powerful awakening. Her gargoyle had transformed into a very aroused and passionate man.

Tenderly, he lowered her to the mossy carpet beneath a grove of large oaks. The coolness of dew clung to her bare ass, creating a new erotic sensation. Excited quivers gripped her. She must take him inside her, now! She wrapped her arms and legs around him, reaching for his kiss. It was only a brief brush of his lips, not at all what she wanted. A deep, husky moan escaped her as he trailed tiny kisses down to where her blouse lay open and flicked his tongue between her breasts, heaving high above the lace bra. He wasted no time pulling the thin shirt from her. In one movement, he released her bra with an expertise that proved he was able to do things no mortal man could.

Her full breasts fell free and large male hands cupped them to his lips, licking each nipple until it hardened. Teasing the excited peaks with his tongue, nibbling and sucking one after the other, he released a satisfied groan. Intense flares of delight raced through her. Knowing she pleased him heightened her arousal. She writhed for release, longing for that familiar sensation to race up her spine and burst into waves of satisfaction. Aggressively, she closed her fingers around his hard cock.

Hot, big and throbbing beneath her touch, he moaned as she stroked him, pumping him. His body stiffened and a low growl vibrated in his chest. His juices slipped from the pink slit and she closed her fingers around the tip of his cock, massaging the come over his foreskin and down his hard shaft. Did he feel the same eagerness as she? He didn't appear to be in any hurry, in fact, he seemed to deliberately draw it out, teasing her, taunting her by withholding the one thing her body screamed for—

"Leonardo," she panted impatiently.

"You are mine, Marcy." His hot breath tunneled into her ear.

A warm chuckle fanned over her breasts as firm lips closed over a nipple. Catching it gently between his teeth, he nibbled and tugged against it. Delightful streaks shot from the erect nipple to her clit. Oh, this teasing must end now!

He planted a series of tiny kisses over her abdomen, pausing to tease her navel with flicks of his tongue. Anticipation roiled in the wake of his teasing, coiling around the tender flesh in her clit, raw and needy.

A low, throaty growl vibrated against her tender flesh as he lowered his head between her legs. She arched to meet his kiss as he spread her legs wider.

His tongue was everywhere, drumming against her clit then slipping to the silky lips of her pussy, plunging inside. She writhed under his artful lovemaking. Fire lashed, with each flicker of his tongue drawing her higher and closer to the climax. She tottered on the edge of sweet release when he moved, leaving her desperate. Before she could protest, he slid between her thighs and the heat of his cock brushed the inside of her leg, leaving a moist streak in its path to her pussy. She guided him to her opening.

"Now, I fulfil your wildest fantasies, Marcy," he promised with a slow penetration, his thrusts thick and hard and deep. Molten juices rushed from her and drenched his cock. Her liquid heat drew him in deeper.

· · ·

It was a powerful sensation. Leonardo had forgotten just how wonderful it was. He rammed his cock deeper into her soft warmth. The walls of her pussy tightened around his swollen cock and he groaned. He would have her. All of her. This woman had stolen his heart night after night, driving him insane with lust and need as she described the many ways she wanted him to make love to her.

"Oh!" she cried out in shuddering ecstasy.

Her excitement drove him beyond thought. Too many nights had he dreamed of fucking her, taking her to the edge of orgasm and bringing her release. He moved in and out of her pussy, creating the needed friction to send her into frenzied undulating, rotating her hips, reaching, longing for the orgasm only he could bring her. He could tell by the quickened rotating of her hips that she needed more. The blood pumped harder and hotter to his cock with each thrust.

He traced hungry kisses along the gentle curve of her neck. She had heard him, and somehow, through his marble prison, he had gained entry into her heart and now she belonged to him, forever. Leonardo ground into her, supporting his hard body slightly above her with palms planted on the mossy ground. His chest brushed against her breasts. The friction of his flesh against her nipples stimulated her into a frenzied urgency. She gripped his buttocks and pushed against him harder, grinding him deeper into her. Her need vibrated between her lips in a slight whimper.

"Leonardo." She gasped for breath.

Her arousal inflamed him and he quickened the rhythm. He'd wanted her for so long. Trapped in his stone prison, unable to take her in his arms, unable to bring her the satisfaction she craved, the release for which he ached. Here she was in his arms, his cock deep inside her and he wanted more. He wanted all of her. The savage, urgent need to bring her to orgasm and to come with her drove him harder. His cock thrust inside her, the walls of her pussy firm and tight, clenching his stiffness, pulling him deeper.

She was the one who had brought him back to life long before tonight. She had sparked the fire in his belly and taught him what desire was. What it was to need the feel of a woman beneath him. She belonged to him now and he intended to leave his mark on her so no other man could ever taste her.

His fingers brushed her cheek, trailing to her flowing hair. She was so beautiful with fire blazing in her eyes—fire he had stoked to life. His fingers threaded in her hair and he tugged and pulled her head back, exposing her slender neck to his taste. He touched his tongue to her neck. His heart slammed against his chest. She tasted just as he knew she would. Sweet and sultry. He flattened his tongue against her soft flesh and licked her neck, raking his tongue into the channel of her ear, nibbling her earlobe, wanting to taste every inch of her, brand her with his touch.

He was rewarded by her low murmurs and moans. He thrust his cock deeper, driving her to orgasm. She spasmed, shuddering as the walls of her pussy clenched his cock, pulling him deeper, squeezing his juices from him. Her rapid breaths heated against his flesh, leaving his skin tingling under her short pants. She gasped for breath, twisting under the liquid release of her orgasm. Fire burst hotter in his groin, her release setting him ablaze. He reared back and released a primal roar. She was his mate! He couldn't control the transformation any more than he could control the raging fire coursing through him. He felt the long mane lengthen and cascade down his back. As much as he tried to stop it, the urgent need to fuck her overwhelmed everything else. The gargoyle features transformed his face. He glanced down at her, worried she would be frightened.

"Take me harder," she cried. Knowing she had aroused him to such a frenzied need that he could no longer maintain his human form set her burning with renewed urgency. Her hips rolled to match his thrusts and he felt the excitement coursing through her. The same demanding liquid fire that surged through him.

Marcy watched him transform. His forehead furrowed and shifted into short golden fur and continued down the bridge of his nose, shaping into that of a lion yet still very human, still very sexy. His wings unfolded from his back and spread open above him. She lifted her finger to stroke the soft fur, tracing it down the bridge of his nose.

"You're so amazing," she panted, noting the husky tone in her voice. "You're such an animal."

"Do you like?" he asked.

"You're one sexy! I've never been with a gargoyle before."

"I've never been with such an exciting woman," he groaned and thrust deeper. The heat pumped up her spine. She tottered on the edge of orgasm again. Hot and edgy, only to recede and twist away. And then, that raw need rose once more, stronger and sizzling. Her self-control stretched and burned, but she could not prolong the moment any longer. She needed release. She needed him!

His hand slipped between their bodies, gliding along her abdomen. Strong fingers sought her moist heat. Firm fingertips pressed into her clit and moved in rapid strokes.

Her gasp was a hot rasp. At long last, the relief she'd sought seized her.

She tilted her pelvis, crying out as the walls of her pussy clamped around his cock, squeezing the orgasm from him. Sweat rolled down the hollow of his spine. He thrust harder, faster, drawing his cock in and out of her pussy until his body spasmed and she felt him come. He ground into her, his fiery liquid spilling. He shuddered. They collapsed in each other's arms—their bodies sticky. He planted kisses along her cheek, pushing aside dampened locks plastered to her forehead.

He was everything she'd imagined and more. Marcy kneaded the hard muscles, rotating with long lazy strokes of the backs of her hands. Hot kisses interrupted with fast pants as he rocked slowly, still buried deep inside her, sent a cascade of pleasure washing over her. That face needed kissing. She held his face between trembling hands, relishing the hot, salty taste. Groping, threading slender fingers through his long hair, she marveled at how magnificent he was. Every inch of her body was touched, kissed and stroked. At length, he rolled onto his back and pulled her over with him, managing to keep his cock embedded deep inside her. She could feel it still pulsating as she straddled him. Taking a deep breath, she rested her head on his broad chest and listened to his heartbeat—strong and steady. They lay entwined in each other's arms for what seemed an eternity, then drifted off to sleep.

Chapter Four

Marcy startled awake, only to find she was still lying on top of him, although his cock had slipped from her. His gargoyle features had receded. She shifted, resting on one elbow, and stared down at him. He had perfect features— a long strong nose, even-set eyes and a bold chin. His lips were perfect. Sensual and firm. Such a strong face. Such a perfect body. And he was hers. At long last Leonardo was flesh and blood and all man. She no longer tried to reason how it was possible. It just was. Her deepest fantasy had finally come true. Leonardo was a man of flesh and wild passion. She couldn't resist tasting his lips and planted a soft kiss. With an arm wrapped about her, he snuggled her closer, but the late-night breeze chilled her and she reached for the discarded blouse. Drawing it about her, she glanced at him and met his stare. He rewarded her with a sexy, lazy smile.

"Are you satisfied?" he asked and stroked her arm with his forefinger.

"For the moment, but don't you go flying off."

His laughter stirred deep emotions in her. It was like sitting in morning sunlight. She was in love—completely and thoroughly.

"Is this just a one-night thing?" she asked.

"What do you mean?" He lifted her hand to his lips and planted a tender kiss.

"Will you turn back?" She dared not ask the question burning her heart, driving fear into that newfound place of contentment.

"Only during the day."

"Will you be with me then? At night?" She tried to sound nonchalant while every nerve ending in her body awaited his response.

"If you want." He pulled her closer, rewarding her with a long, slow kiss before releasing her lips.

"Oh yes," she gasped for breath, "I want you every night." She encircled her arms around his neck. He was not going to leave her now that he was free.

"Then that is how it shall be," he promised. "You're chilled." He rolled her over, and stretched. The unmistakable sound of wings spreading out filled the air. He shifted and wrapped them around her, creating the same warmth as if he'd covered her with a blanket and cocooned her to him.

"What about the witch?" She nuzzled into his neck, dreading to break the enchanting moment, but she must know.

"When I was created, I was meant to remain on my perch forever. So an incantation was made and there I've remained. Even when I was moved from Romania to Italy to New York and then to Atlanta." He nibbled her ear.

"So it *was* a spell. I wasn't just imagining it. You're real."

"Did you not find my lovemaking real?" He flicked his tongue into her ear, playing a drumming staccato that vibrated all the way to the wet heat between her legs.

"It was better than real." She slid from him, placing eager kisses all over his muscular body until she wrapped her fingers around his stiff cock and covered him with her lips, taking him deep into her mouth. She rolled her tongue around his cock, enjoying the way its velvety flesh felt against it. His thickness filled her mouth. She pulled the foreskin back to circle her tongue over the exposed crown. He groaned and moved his hips, thrusting his cock deeper into her mouth. His reaction aroused her further and she pushed him onto his back. He collapsed with a deep sigh of contentment as she stroked him, rubbing her hand up his length and grasping the end of his cock. Pearls of semen moistened her hand and she leaned over to trace tiny circles around his erection with her tongue, lapping his juices until he growled and turned her onto her stomach.

Heat flamed and licked at them beneath the canopy of his wings. She rose onto unsteady knees with an anxious fluttering in her stomach as she thrust her hips up to receive his large cock. Instead, he moved between her legs, licking his fingers then spreading the moistness over her opening and slid them inside her. Liquid heat rushed from her. His breathing was labored. She was moist and ready for him and he thrust his cock into her. His grip tightened and he pulled her hard against him. His hot throbbing cock filled her completely.

"Oh, don't wait, Leonardo," her voice trembled. She needed him to take her hard and fast and that's just what he did, not needing any further encouragement. His balls slapped against her as his hands grasped her hips, pulling her into him. Firm fingertips teased her swollen clit. Wild, searing energy coiled up her spine, lashing in molten waves.

The sensations rose up her spine. She shuddered with the burst of pleasure. Brilliant shards of light filled her vision followed by the uncontrollable quivering as she came hard and quickly. He pounded his cock harder into her, gripping her hips, drawing her along his length. She moaned when his body went rigid.

He shuddered with the spasms, rotating his hips. She collapsed onto the moss bed, her hips still poised against him as he pulsed with fiery wetness slipping around him. Turning slightly onto his side, he pulled her down into his arms and held her. She clamped her muscles around his cock, delighting in the new series of pulses she drew from him.

"I love you, Marcy," he whispered hoarsely in her ear. Her eyes fluttered open.

She twisted her neck to kiss him, but needed to feel his chest against her breasts and eased from him, letting his cock, wet and slick with their combined juices, slide from her. It was easy to push him onto his back and lie on top of him. His kiss was hungry with promises of more. He possessed her, taking her tongue captive with his. Finally she broke from him, gasping.

"I love you, Leonardo. I've loved you since the first day I saw you, even though I knew it was absurd to fall in love with a statue. But I couldn't help it. And I have so many questions."

"All you have to do is ask." He stroked her face. "Every day I watched you work and called out to you. And when you talked to me about your dreams and how much you wanted me, I knew you were the one to free me. I told you my name over and over and then one day, you called me Leonardo. Somehow you heard me. I knew we would be together forever."

"But I'm mortal," she sighed and buried her face in his shoulder.

"Only if you wish."

"W-What do you mean?" Her pulse quickened.

"You can be like me, if you desire."

"A gargoyle?" The thought took root and wound itself around her heart, tugging against all the reasons she could think of not to become like him.

"You can transform."

"How? I mean—"

"It's another way to make love. I must divide. It's difficult to explain and better demonstrated."

"Divide? As in becoming two men?"

"I can do it only once, but once is all it takes."

"Oh my!" Excitement coursed through her, setting up an erratic drumming pulse. Two Leonardos making love to her. Dare she even think about it? The mere thought nearly made her come.

"There would be two of me. One for each . . . opening."

"Anal sex?"

He nodded, looking down at her, running the back of his hand over her cheek.

"And that's it? That will transform me into a gargoyle?"

"As long as the three of us come at the same time."

"It sounds complicated." She didn't add "extremely exciting beyond her wildest fantasies."

"It's a ritual, my love, not complicated. A mere act of supreme love. You only have to wish and I shall make it so." He didn't tell her the rest. He couldn't. Not yet. She must become his mate by free will. If she knew it was the only way to free him of part of the witch's curse that had entrapped him as a statue, then Marcy would do it for that reason alone. He wanted her. He wanted his freedom, but he loved her too much to use tricks.

"Everything's happening so quickly. It sounds absolutely wonderful to have two of you." She nestled deeper in his embrace.

"You don't have to decide right now. But soon. The opportunity will be gone when the sun rises."

"Forever?" She stiffened in his arms.

"Forever." He tightened his embrace. He must prepare her for the truth—later.

Leonardo wrapped his wings around her, reveling in the sensation of being alive. The joy crushed with the realization he might lose Marcy and his freedom. He held her, basking in the way she felt next to him. Her touch had the most disarming effect. He would do anything to protect her. Anything. Even if it meant going back to his perch for all eternity. He had longed to be free but now that he was, it meant her life was in danger. It was too big a risk. He should have known the witch would find them soon after the spell was broken.

"Oh Leonardo," she moaned. "What have I done? I've placed you in danger."

"Shh, my love. You're safe." He stroked her hair. "In my hunger for you, I could only think of taking you. Making you mine. I'm so sorry."

She turned in his arms to face him.

"I don't care about anything other than you, Leonardo. I want to be your mate." Her voice trembled.

"You don't know what you're saying." He stroked her cheek, longing to believe it was possible.

"You're such a part of me, even before the spell was broken. I was destined to be with you," she sighed.

"But your family, your friends—"

"I don't have any family. And Nel, my assistant, is the only friend I have. No one will miss me, Leonardo. I want you to perform the ritual now." Her lips spread into a smile—a smile that ripped through his resolve and struck his heart like a branding iron.

"Then we must hurry before the sun rises." His heartbeat felt as though it would burst with the emotion filling him. She loved him! Enough to sacrifice her mortal life and spend eternity with him as a gargoyle. With his love by his side forever—it was too much to believe. He ran his hand through his hair and glanced at her.

"I'm ready."

She offered him freedom! Her selfless act brought greater gain to him than she could imagine. He would be free of the spell that had bound him to a perch for centuries. He would have the life of a gargoyle. Stone by day and man by night. Together, he and Marcy would rule the night.

"What will happen? Will it be p-painful for you to divide?"

"Your transformation will be one made of love, my sweet. Only joy and pleasure. I promise." He kissed her forehead. "Let us begin."

The night grew soft and welcoming. A serenade of crickets and tree fogs filled the summer night, all lit by the brilliant starlight that seemed to surround them.

"I'm nervous," she admitted, not knowing what to expect, mindful that an enraged witch searched for them.

"Can the witch fly, Leonardo?"

"She cannot. She's bound to the earth by her wickedness. She can scry for us, but she'll arrive too late. That's why I brought us to this mountain. It's not easily accessible. Once her claim on me is severed, she can never harm me again. Nor can she harm my mate. I shall remain a gargoyle as will you for all eternity. Unfortunately, that part of her spell cannot be broken." His voice was deep and husky.

"I'm ready, Leonardo. I am not afraid to be transformed."

Electrical pulses shot through her. Excited anticipation of the ritual drew her breath from her. He stepped from their embrace and she ached for his touch.

"Now I shall divide, so I can make you mine."

Chapter Five

er heartbeat pounded in her chest. Bathed in moonlight, standing naked in front of her, was the man of her deepest desires. And she was going to have two of him.

She quivered from the rush of excitement coursing through her. Tall and strong with powerful muscles flexing and rippling his tanned skin, Leonardo was perfect. She swallowed against the building heat. Aroused and needing to feel him inside her, Marcy clasped sweaty hands together and let her stare move over him. His six-pack was defined and toned all the way to his trim waist. She lowered her stare to his large cock, erect and pulsating. Could she manage two of him? Leonardo rounded his shoulders and leaned over in a crouching position. Straining every muscle in his body, he transformed into a gargoyle once more. Half-man, half-lion.

She took a step back just as he raised his head and

released a fierce roar. It blasted and swirled down into her
ears as though entering her body and traveling to her abdomen. The sound echoed from the mountaintop over the valley
below.

Fascinated yet apprehensive, she trembled, not daring to
move. She watched him straighten and once more take human
form, only a full-sized lion remained at his feet. Her breath
escaped in a rush. The lion straightened, transforming into a
duplicate male shape.

Her pulse throbbed and her breath came in short, fast
waves. Two of him! A tingling sensation moved from her
hardened nipples to her clit. A scorching fervor burned away
all remaining fears. This was something she definitely wanted!
Wet heat rushed from her as she stood waiting. Not knowing
what to do next.

"Come, my love. Let us please you." He held out his hand
and stepped around the duplicate.

"Can he speak?"

"No." Leonardo drew her into his embrace. "But he can
do what he needs to do, which is all I require. I hope he will
please you."

"O-Oh." She gulped, looking down at the duplicate's stiff
cock. "I'm sure he will. Can I call him Leo?" she asked and
Leonardo nodded.

"Come, join us," he spoke to the duplicate and the man
followed.

She trembled when the duplicate moved behind her. Leonardo drew her into his embrace and captured her lips, stifling
the question she was about to ask. It was soon answered when
the duplicate touched her back, running his hands down to
her waist. He stooped down behind her to plant tender wet

kisses over her buttocks. Delightful tingles and goose bumps
cascaded over her.

Leonardo's kiss deepened and she squirmed against the liquid heat rushing from her pussy, drenching her thighs. Warm
hands, large and confident, cupped her buttocks, kneading
them gently. Her senses sparked from every direction. Leonardo
ran his hand over her breasts, taking turns to roll and squeeze
a nipple between his thumb and forefinger. She writhed under
the intense sensations coursing to her pussy.

The duplicate behind her slipped his hands between her
legs and spread them wide so that she locked her knees, bracing herself. She startled when his fingers slipped between the
silken lips of her shaved pussy and rubbed her clit. She gasped
beneath Leonardo's kiss as the other man's tongue flicked
against her swollen clit. Leonardo planted kisses down her
neck to her breasts and captured an erect nipple between his
lips, supporting her with his arm behind her back. She leaned
backwards.

Fingers probed the opening of her pussy with short
tongue lashes growing stronger. Leo's fingers plunged inside
her and moved in and out. Another finger, moist and slick
with his saliva, toyed in circular motions around her anus
until finally probing tenderly inside. Pleasurable sensations
rippled through her. Panting from Leonardo's suckling, she
spread her legs wider, allowing the other man greater access.
She was rewarded with a deeper thrust into her pussy. Hands
were everywhere, squeezing her nipples, thrusting inside her
pussy, and now the added sensation inside her asshole. She
moaned and writhed under their hand-play.

The thrusts inside her pussy quickened with Leo's tongue
dancing over her clit, teasing and licking until the tingling

sensations changed, surging in heated spikes up her spine to her head and burst in shards of extreme delight. The walls of her pussy clamped around Leo's fingers and her clit throbbed beneath the tip of his tongue. A sensual heat bathed her with tender nerve endings quivering in anticipation. Wetness trickled from her pussy, damp from his teasing. Her anus clenched against his finger, pushing another orgasm to burst in her like a wildfire.

Moaning, she felt she would collapse under the intense pleasure. Leonardo must have sensed this for he drew his arms tighter around her and said something to his duplicate. The thick finger gingerly pulled from her anus, but the fingers inside her pussy remained. His lips closed over her clit and sucked, sending her body into another powerful spasm.

"Release her," Leonardo commanded harshly and the duplicate pulled his fingers from inside her and groaned as he moved from her.

Leonardo lifted her in his arms. Groggy from the overwhelming sensations of such extreme pleasure, Marcy formed the words as he carried her over to the lush bed of moss. "D-Do you feel what he does?" she slurred.

"Oh yes." His breath was ragged and labored. Sweat beaded along his brow and she knew it had taken great control for him not to take her in the heat of her own orgasm.

"Lie here, my love, and let us give you more pleasure."

"I don't know if I can take it. It was so intense. So wonderful."

"Enjoy this night, Marcy. I cannot give it to you ever again."

"I have every intention of enjoying it." She lifted onto her elbows and looked past him to the duplicate obediently waiting behind him.

"Come here, Leo," she ordered and he obediently knelt in front of her. She sat up and glanced back at Leonardo. "I want you to watch me with him." She caught Leonardo's stare and sensed the rush of excitement coursing through him. His lips formed a sexy, lopsided grin.

Marcy let her fingertips trace the thin line of hair from his navel to his cock. Leo grinned when she pushed him down onto the mossy bed and took his cock in her mouth. She sucked on it, stealing a glance at Leonardo who stood with his hand around his cock, stroking as he watched. Knowing he watched her and could feel what she did to his duplicate was one of the most arousing moments she'd ever experienced. Her clit throbbed, aching for his touch, but this time it would be all about Leo. She licked the tip of his cock, twirling her tongue around the heated, moist shaft, drawing him into her mouth, sucking and molding her mouth around his hardness. She moved up and down his length.

Leo groaned and held her head between his hands. The groan beside her assured her Leonardo was enjoying her strokes as well. She sensed him close to climax and slowed the rhythm, releasing him from her mouth, still gliding her hands over him. She stole a side-glance and met Leonardo's fierce passion-filled look.

"Do you enjoy watching me?" She straddled Leo, guiding his cock inside her. Leonardo moved around her, so he now stood a few feet from the duplicate's head.

"You're so beautiful." His words were hoarse and deep. He rubbed his hand up and down his cock as she rode Leo, sliding her pussy up and down his heated shaft, driving him deeper inside her each time. Leonardo growled and fell to his knees beside them.

"I want you." He lowered his head to capture a nipple between his lips, but she tugged from his suckling. He stroked his cock faster.

"Here." She shoved his hand aside and wrapped her fingers around him, moving her hand up and down his shaft.

"I love you." He lifted his face and leaned back with his hands planted beside him, supporting himself as she masturbated him.

Leo grabbed her hips and lifted her up and down his cock, faster. The movement forced her to release Leonardo's cock and he growled, leaning over his duplicate.

"She belongs to me!" He lifted her from the duplicate who roared and lunged for Leonardo. "Enough," he said, holding up his hand, and the other man backed away, settling down onto the moss once more.

"What just happened?" she asked, feeling the anger between the two men, wondering if she'd done something wrong.

"He grows stronger in his lust for you. We should not wait any longer for your transformation."

"What would happen?"

"He might refuse to merge back into me."

"What?" The thought took root. "I could have two of you always?"

"Only one of us would live, Marcy. Let us continue with the ritual. Lie down, my love." He guided her beside the duplicate who stretched out beside her and teased her nipple with his tongue while his hand glided to her pussy.

Leonardo settled between her legs, pushing the duplicate's hand away. His tongue flickered against her clit, drumming against her rising heat. The duplicate seized her lips and drew her, into a passionate kiss. His hands groped her breasts and pinched her nipples, drawing a groan from her. She rolled her head to one side and saw a thin streak of light along the mountain peaks. It would be sunrise soon.

"Lie down," Leonardo commanded the duplicate, who obeyed.

Leonardo then lifted her from the ground and held her suspended over the duplicate. Leo grasped her buttocks and spread them. She stiffened when his tongue flickered against her anus, but quickly relaxed against the tiny circles he created, teasing and plunging inside the outer rim. Would he fuck her now? Or was he teasing her still? She wanted him. Wanted both of them. She was crazy with desire and moaned, arching her hips to receive his tongue as Leonardo supported her.

Slowly, Leonardo moved her lower so she was positioned against Leo's cock. Moistness greeted her butt cheeks and the tip of his cock teased her anus. She tried to relax her muscles, knowing without a lubricant it would be painful. Sudden warmth of his cock's juices flowed over her opening and lubricated his entry. She sensed his excitement and admired his control as he penetrated. His cock seemed to narrow, making the entry easy. He took it slow, allowing her time to relax against him. Once inside, he seemed to expand but still not to his full size, for which she was grateful.

"There now, lie back on top of him and spread your legs. He'll support you," Leonardo instructed, parting her legs wider so he could slide into her pussy.

"How can—?"

"Remember? I told you it's a ritual. Magic helps make things easier. Especially his part. He's a magical being of sorts.

His cock narrows whenever it becomes too intense for you. He'll know. Can sense it. He won't hurt you. We shall be aware of him, but you shouldn't hold back because he can diminish in size easily should you need him to—"

"I want you, Leonardo. Take me so I can be your mate." The sensation of Leo's cock inside her ass was unlike anything she'd ever felt. With Leonardo's cock fully inside her pussy, the two sensations heightened her arousal to the point she was on the edge of orgasm. She worried she would come before him and then the transformation would not happen. She sensed Leo also tottered on the edge of orgasm as he supported her with his body with his arms wrapped around her.

Leonardo moved against her and to her surprise, Leo seemed to reduce and expand his cock with each movement so instead of the expected pain, it was the most arousing sensation she'd ever felt.

The feeling of both men inside her was so intense, her clit throbbed and her pussy clamped hard against Leonardo with her anus clenching under the orgasm. Had she come too soon?

Leo moved under her, lifting her up slightly and bringing her back down, while Leonardo supported himself on his hands and slid in and out of her pussy.

"Stop," he ordered his twin.

Leo growled and reluctantly obeyed. She could feel him pulsing in her. A new wave of arousal rose and she rotated her hips, grinding into both men. The erotic waves rose higher. Excited sensations tingled and tantalized her in waves of pleasure. Leo moved under her again, ignoring Leonardo's warning. She moved faster. The men followed her rhythm, Leonardo thrusting his cock deeper into her pussy.

The heated excitement snaked up her spine, pulsating and rising toward orgasm. Every nerve ending was teased to the edge of release. She gasped and quivered under the sudden burst of energy. The orgasm gripped her, clenching her anus around Leo's cock while the walls of her pussy grasped Leonardo's cock.

"Leonardo!" she cried out. Leo groaned underneath her in response to the hard clamping down on his cock. His come spilled into her just as Leonardo went rigid under the powerful orgasm gripping him. He growled and hot liquid rushed inside her.

Sweating and panting, the three of them were a throbbing mass of tangled arms and legs. She lay on top of Leo, with Leonardo on top of her. It was difficult in that split second to know where she ended and the two men began. Her back was plastered to Leo's chest. Her breasts were plastered to Leonardo's. A deep warmth moved from her stomach to her chest, tingling to her hardened nipples. The ritual was complete. She'd never felt so satiated.

"Leonardo," she gasped. Had it worked? Was she now a gargoyle? She didn't feel any different. How was a gargoyle supposed to feel? She tightened her arms around his neck and licked a salty trail up his neck to his lips.

Panting, he sucked her lower lip into his mouth and teased it with his tongue and then released it. He pressed a kiss on her forehead.

Suddenly, the fullness in her anus disappeared and so did Leo.

She cried out as she fell to the ground with Leonardo still inside her. He caught himself and slipped from her, rolling sideways onto the mossy carpet.

Marcy giggled and crawled on top of him, scattering kisses over his tufted chest. She followed the thin line of hair to his navel with the tip of her tongue. He twisted under her tickling and gathered her into his arms. She rested her chin on his chest and stared at him.

"How do you feel?" he asked.

"Very satisfied. Should I feel something . . . gargoylish?"

He chuckled and nestled her against him. "Not yet. You will not become gargoyle until sunrise, my love. You will feel it then."

The blissful moment shattered. A woman's laughter pierced the quiet night like a clap of thunder, chilling Marcy's very soul. She tore from his embrace, turning in time to see a woman dressed in slacks and a cotton top standing over them with hands on hips. Fading moonlight struck her face and Marcy gasped. The woman was beautiful. She had long flowing golden hair and delicate features. Not at all how she'd envisioned the witch who had imprisoned Leonardo.

"Your whore shall die, Leonardo. And you will return to your perch for all eternity," she seethed.

"Your powers are no longer a threat to me, Lyria."

The witch raised her arm and pointed her finger at him.

"Stone you were, stone you are for all eternity. I command you back to your perch." A bolt of blue jagged lightning shot from her fingertip to him.

Marcy screamed but Leonardo laughed. What was wrong with him? The streak of light moved toward him but deflected as though hitting an invisible barrier. The brilliant blue ricocheted and bounced back to the witch. It struck her full force. Her scream pierced the night, and a grayness moved over her, flesh hardening as the current coursed through her, freezing her in an eternal stone image of surprise and anger.

"W-What happened?" Marcy asked. She pressed against Leonardo. His powerful body was a shield between her and the statue. She stared in horror at the woman who was now stone. The witch's mouth was locked into a twisted scream with fear and anger creasing her face.

"She's been destroyed." Leonardo gathered her into his arms. "By transforming, you broke her spell."

"I did? But why didn't you tell me that before I made the choice?"

"I wanted you to make the choice out of love. Your desire to be with me. And now you have freed us." He planted a kiss on her lips.

"The sun—Leonardo." She pointed at the light rising over the ridge.

"We shall awaken together when it sets this evening. We will be as we are now, man and woman. It's only during the day that we'll appear as gargoyles." He clasped her hand in his.

His touch eased her panic as the rays of light fell over them and she felt her skin hardening. Her heart pounded harder. His fingers tightened around her hand and her fear subsided. Come night, she would be with her Leonardo again. Forever. He spread his wings about them. Marcy felt her back muscles tense and wings emerge from her flesh. Her wings.

"I would wish to spend the day in your arms." She curled against him.

"And I with my lips against yours, my love. Until tonight." He lowered his face to hers and seized her lips with his just as the sun rose over the mountainside and sealed them together in stone.

Tall, Dark and Deadly

MARGARET L. CARTER

Chapter One

he air hummed with rapt attention from dozens of human minds, most of them female. "Oh, lady bright! Can it be right—This window open to the night?" Claude paused in his recitation to savor the shallow breaths and rapid heartbeats of his audience, inaudible to human ears but plain to his. He had performed this reading of Poe's "The Sleeper" so often that it required only a fraction of his attention. He knew just what phrases to linger over to coax the most intense emotions from the listeners.

Their fascination perfumed the air like a cloud of incense. He could almost taste it, a delicious appetizer for the more substantial feast he anticipated enjoying later that night. For the black-clad young women he half-affectionately thought of as "vampire groupies," he knew his hypnotic delivery transformed the drab hotel function room into a boudoir "beneath the mystic moon" with an "opiate vapour, dewy, dim." While he didn't believe Poe had written "The Sleeper" with a vampire's nocturnal visit in mind, doubtless the "window open to the night" conjured up just that image for most of the audience, a reaction that suited Claude very well.

His eyes swept over the group while he intoned, "Oh, lady, dear, hast thou no fear? Why and what art thou dreaming here?" Locking glances briefly with each female in the first couple of rows, he savored the way a blush blossomed on each one's face at the fantasy that he addressed the lines to her alone. About midway to the back of the room though he captured the eyes of one person who watched him with peculiar intensity, a woman of about thirty with mahogany hair pulled back in a braid. From her he sensed a hunger that answered his own with a more complicated need than the yearning for a fantasy vampire's bite.

Pleasantly rounded from what he could see of her, though not enough to violate the current standards for female beauty, she had what people used to call a "peaches and cream" complexion. Claude approved of her apparent refusal to either diet herself into emaciation or bake her skin under cancer-inducing rays. She would make an excellent dessert. The image made his jaws ache.

He mentally shook himself. He already had plans for tonight. Still, it wouldn't hurt to make contact with her and keep her in reserve, so to speak. Winding up the poem, he smiled at the memory of a lapel pin he'd seen on one of the fans earlier that day: "Cthulhu Saves—He Might Get Hungry Later."

He stood up with a flourish of his cape to signal the end of the session. Instantly, the audience mobbed the front of the

room, convention programs and pens in hand. Teeth clenched
in the closest thing to a smile he could manage, he scribbled
his name as requested, watching the back of the delectable
woman's head vanish into the corridor. With all the people
blocking his view, he hadn't even managed a glimpse of her
name tag.

Finally, dry-mouthed with thirst from exposure to his fans'
body heat, pulse sounds and keyed-up emotions, he broke away
and headed for his room. Though he lived only a few blocks
away, his need for a refuge in the middle of the convention
made renting a hotel room worthwhile. He craved a few hours
of sleep before that evening's awards banquet.

When he unlocked the door, he noticed an unfamiliar
scent. His nostrils flared. Not human, but acrid and quasi-
metallic, like one of his own kind. Something rustled under
his feet as the door closed behind him. A large manila envelope.

Tossing the cape onto the bed, he took the envelope to the
desk and opened it. Two newspaper clippings fell out. Both, he
saw, came from a San Francisco paper. The first headline read,
"Human Remains Discovered Under Church Parking Lot."

About a month earlier, archaeologists had begun excavat-
ing that parking lot in downtown San Francisco in preparation
for expansion of St. Anthony's parish hall. Inside the buried
ruins of the original church building, destroyed in the 1906
earthquake, searchers had found two bodies. Oddly, one, a
woman's, had been reduced to a skeleton, yet the other was
remarkably preserved, as lifelike as the famous Inca maiden
sacrifices. That mummified corpse was a man's.

Claude's heart raced. He had to concentrate to force it
under control. He was annoyed to discover his hand shaking as

he picked up the second clipping. "Earthquake Mummy Vanishes." The bodies had been turned over to the anthropology department at the University of California, Berkeley. Two days after being transported there—more like two nights, Claude suspected—the man's corpse had vanished. Claude knew the "corpse" had never been truly lifeless though and he wasn't surprised to read of the security guard found dead in the hallway outside the storage vault.

So Philip was alive. Not only alive, but here in Los Angeles at this very hotel. He had obviously shoved the envelope under the door of Claude's room within the past couple of hours. *He's after me. Wonder what the devil he wants? Revenge, no doubt, but what kind?*

He flashed on a memory of the ground shaking and the church roof caving in, while Philip howled in anguish over the maimed body of his woman.

Picking up the phone, Claude dialed the Prime Elder's number. If the Council didn't already know about Philip's resurrection, they needed to. Claude heaved an exasperated sigh at the vanished prospect for a decent afternoon's sleep.

Panting from her run to the elevator, Eloise Kern dashed into her hotel room and flung herself onto the bed. She'd meant to introduce herself to Claude Darvell after the poetry reading, but her reaction to his resonant voice and penetrating gaze had embarrassed her so much she couldn't face him. Especially after that moment when she'd imagined his eyes had lingered on her a bit longer than on anyone else.

Oh, stop thinking like a ditzy fan! she scolded herself. Every female in that room had doubtless imagined the same thing. She hadn't come here to indulge in fantasies about her favorite horror movie star. She'd wheedled her friend on the con committee into seating Claude next to her at the awards banquet so she could conduct business, not drool over his ebony hair and violet-gray eyes. Keeping her mind on screenplay contracts would have been a lot easier if he'd looked less ravishing in person than on film instead of more so.

For weeks since receiving his latest letter, she'd had to read it over and over to confirm she hadn't imagined it. She'd even packed it in her overnight bag for reassurance. By now she knew the relevant passages by heart, from "Dear Ms. Kern" to "I look forward to discussing your proposed adaptation of *Varney the Vampyre* in person at ConCatastrophe." She peeled off her clothes and stepped under a hot shower, lost in visions of Claude—"tall, dark and deadly," as a tabloid reporter had labeled him—emoting the lines from her own script.

She visualized him in the opening scene taken directly from the novel, climbing through a window on a moonlit night, like the one in the poem, to plunge his fangs into the heroine's delicate throat. Eloise's nipples puckered at the image. Throwing her head back, with her eyes closed, she let the warm water flow over her own neck, imagining his lips fastened there. *There you go again, like a teenybopper with a crush,* she mocked herself.

Better to wallow in that daydream than to brood over the other letter, the one she'd stuffed in her purse right before leaving home. The home she might not have much longer. The management of her townhouse complex had spent the past few months planning a conversion from rentals to a condominium regime. Eloise had started saving toward the down payment and closing costs, a slow process between her mother's nursing home fees and the uncertainty of a writer's income, but she hadn't expected the shift from rental to condo for another couple of years. Suddenly the schedule had accelerated. She had six months to dredge up the money or get out. Guild minimum for a screenplay would make the difference between home ownership and homelessness.

Wrenching the shower knob to the "off" position, she toweled dry with impatient roughness, threw on a robe and sat at the dresser to brush her hair and redo the French braid. Why was she imagining herself as a bag lady? Multi-published authors with doctorates in English lit didn't end up on the street. She gave her hair a last, firm twist and looped a scrunchy around the end. Enough negative vibes! She had to project confidence when she met Claude at the banquet. What actor would want to produce or star in a movie scripted by a writer with the stalwart firmness of a bowl of Jell-O?

Chapter Two

e wasn't coming. The place next to Eloise at the award recipients' table, with "Claude Darvell" on the name card, sat empty. He must have been stricken with a sudden illness or called away on some emergency. Blinking in the atmospheric candlelight, she considered eating his chocolate mousse. Anxiety always made her feel like nibbling, and all the rolls were gone. Sure, she didn't have to meet him in person to negotiate the projected movie deal. But she felt she'd have a much better chance if they could discuss the script face-to-face.

Lost in worry, she clapped automatically after each presentation and almost missed her own name. Recovering, she scurried up to the podium to receive her award for the con committee's pick as author of the year's best paranormal romance. She read her brief acceptance speech off an index card, her own voice echoing hollowly in her ears as if it were somebody else's. Glad to make it back to the table without tripping over her high heels, she didn't register at first that the seat beside her was no longer vacant.

In a black, crimson-lined cape that seemed to add inches to his already imposing height, Claude Darvell stood up to give her a half-bow of greeting. "Eloise? I'm Claude."

"Yes, I know." She cringed internally at the inane remark.

"Congratulations on your award." He clasped her hand briefly. His skin, she noticed, felt cool. A delightful shiver ran up her arm. "Forgive my lateness. I'm afraid I overslept."

She stomped firmly on a fantasy of his dark, wavy hair tousled from the pillow. In person he looked even more like an updated Lord Byron than he did onscreen. "You missed dinner."

Gathering the cape over one arm, he sat down. "I didn't come here for the food." His violet-gray eyes prowled over her before turning toward the speaker on the podium. "I'd like a glass of wine though." He waved at the half-finished bottle of burgundy, which she passed to him.

"There go my illusions," she whispered. "What happened to the 'I never drink wine' bit?"

"After a day at a convention, I'll drink anything," he whispered back, leaning close so that his breath ruffled her hair.

A sensation like the caress of invisible fingers tickled down her back. She sipped her own wine and forced her attention to the next presentation. Minutes later, Claude got up to accept his award for best male lead in a horror film. Eloise watched his panther-like stride with growing appreciation. As far as she could tell with the cape and tux, he had the build of a greyhound, sleek and thin. Far from an illusion of makeup and camera angles, his demon lover persona proved even more captivating face-to-face.

She still had trouble believing her luck, that he had taken the time to write an appreciative letter about her article analyzing his "Count Orloff" vampire movies in the *Journal of Popular Culture*. Still more incredibly, her note of thanks in reply had elicited another message from him, and they'd become regular correspondents. When she had mentioned her half-finished script based on that sprawling Victorian penny-dreadful novel, *Varney the Vampyre*, Claude had expressed his own long-standing desire to film the novel. So here they were, sharing a bottle of burgundy and the hopes of making a movie together.

When the master of ceremonies finished his concluding remarks, Claude turned to her. "Did you bring any of your *Varney* material with you?"

Of course she had, though she wouldn't have committed the faux pas of pressing it on him without an invitation. "Yes, I've got a proposal and a partial script." Thanks to her past dealings with producers who had optioned a few of her books, she had enough familiarity with the workings of Hollywood to prepare such things in the proper format.

"I'd love to take a look at them." Pulling out her chair, he lightly clasped her wrist, as if taking her pulse.

Bracing herself against the prickle of sensation that danced along the inside of her arm, she told herself he wasn't doing that at all. Or if he was, the gesture was only part of the vampire pose he assumed for the entertainment of his fans. "Great, let's go up to my room," she said, hoping the invitation didn't sound like a come-on. Not that she would have minded if he'd taken the words as an opening for seduction, but if she wanted to deal with him on a business level, she'd better not mix her signals.

On the way to the elevator, Claude's hand rested on her back at her waistline. When they'd touched before, she'd thought his skin felt cool. How could it burn her through the satin of her evening gown? By the time the elevator started ascending to her floor, she already felt lightheaded. *I'm just nervous about the script,* she thought. That was the only reason for her rapid pulse. Sure.

"I noticed you at the reading earlier," he said as they walked down the sixth-floor corridor.

"I didn't want to try to introduce myself in the middle of that crowd," she fibbed. To her annoyance, her hand shook when she tried to insert the key. Inside, she switched on the foyer light and one of the reading lamps.

"That's plenty," he said before she could turn on any others. He stepped over to the window and gazed at the sparkling skyline, with the famous illuminated "Hollywood" sign on a distant hillside. "It's a beautiful night. As beautiful as downtown Los Angeles ever gets, anyhow." He punctuated the remark with a wry smile.

"Yeah, I haven't seen a night this smog-free in ages." Eloise took the treatment and script out of her briefcase and handed them to Claude.

"Oh, yes, you live nearby."

"Pasadena. But I'd rather pay for a room than drive home after midnight two nights in a row."

"I share your sentiments," he said, leafing through the printout she'd given him. "I have a penthouse just a few blocks away on Wilshire." He set the pages on the desk and drew her to the window with a casual touch at her waist. "I'll read all this later. Right now, I'd rather hear the highlights straight from you."

"Sure." She froze, half wishing he wouldn't touch her so that she could keep her mind on Victorian vampires and half wishing he'd make that touch more than casual. Her nipples peaked, creating friction with the lining of her bra, and her stomach fluttered. "I'm sorry I don't have anything to drink I can offer you."

"Don't worry about that. I'm not thirsty—right now." His hand drifted from her waist to her neck, skimming the bare skin above the low-cut dress on the way. His fingers insinuated under the braid and gently rubbed the roots of her hair. "Are you planning to have me commit suicide in Mount Vesuvius, the way the book ends?"

"Sure. Think of the cool special effects." She tried to focus on a vampire diving into a volcano instead of the heat that swirled around her scalp and down her spine.

He chuckled. "More hot than cool, *n'est-ce pas?*"

"Ha, ha. Don't most vampires attack with fangs, not puns?"

"I suppose we can't do without fangs. Audiences expect them. Speaking of attacks, we'll start the film with Varney invading Flora's bedroom?"

"Of course. The first scene of the book is too good to waste. Hail, thunder, wind, lightning and a demon of the night feasting on a half-naked girl. Starting and ending will be the easy part. The hard part is deciding what to do with the other eight hundred pages in between." She tilted her head, the better to enjoy his gentle rubbing. She felt like a cat having its ears scratched.

"I'm sure you'll work it out. I do look forward to playing

jolly old blood-and-thunder Varney, as long as we don't make him one of those undead twits who constantly whines about the terrible curse he's under."

"Perish the thought." She caught herself leaning back against the hard length of Claude's torso. His massage, moving from her hairline to her shoulder blades, made her want to purr. *I really should make him stop that.*

"Handled properly," he said, "Varney could be a new twist on the tragic vampire. New to the box office public, anyway, since nobody reads the book except specialists like you. I have a couple of financial backers in mind. Once I've got a general idea of the plot outline, I'll contact them and set up the deal."

The conversation was progressing faster than Eloise had dared hope. She knew Claude, even though his official biography said he was independently wealthy, wouldn't put up the funding himself. No sensible actor/producer would violate Hollywood's "OPM" rule—use Other People's Money. The fact that he'd already considered the financing issue showed he was serious. She murmured a wordless sound of agreement. Why did she feel so fuzzy around the edges? She hadn't consumed that much wine at dinner. Why did Claude's touch seem to scorch right through her clothes? She'd never responded to a man so intensely, not even one who embodied her deepest fantasies.

"Very well, I break into Flora's chamber in the middle of a storm. What's my motivation? Other than my appetite for her nubile flesh and sweet blood, of course?"

His breath ruffled Eloise's hair. Her pulse pounded in her temples, and she felt her face flush. "The house," she said, trying to catch her breath. "He left England in the seventeenth century, when he turned into a vampire after Cromwell's men killed him. Now he's back, and the Bannerworths are living in his mansion.

He's tired of wandering and thinks he can find peace in his ancestral home. He wants to scare them into selling it."

"Is Flora frightened of him?" Claude's hands moved to her upper arms and stroked up and down, making the bare skin prickle with heat. He seemed to savor the sensual motion as much as she did.

"At first. Who wouldn't be, with a man crashing in through her window? Not to mention a man with fangs and claws and glittering, silver eyes."

"Hold on, the book says his eyes look like polished tin."

"Never mind that," Eloise said, her breath coming shallow and fast. "It's my script, and I don't think polished tin sounds very romantic."

"Oh, so you want a romantic vampire?" A hint of soft laughter underlay the remark.

She blushed still hotter. "You've read my stuff. You know what kind of vampire I like." She'd sent him autographed copies of a couple of her novels, and his reply had made it plain that he'd done more with the books than glance at the title pages.

"Will this film have an R rating? Where will Varney pierce Flora's tender skin? Here?" To Eloise's surprise, he bent to kiss the side of her neck with a butterfly-wing flicker of his tongue. "Or here?" One fingertip traced a line from the hollow of her throat to the swell of her right breast above the V of her gown.

Her heart raced. A melting sensation flowed from the spot where his touch lingered to the hollow between her legs. She forced a deep breath and said, "I think you'd better leave."

He flung off the cloak and draped it over a chair, then removed his bow tie and tossed it on the desk. "I'll leave when I'm good and ready," he said in a tone of genial firmness. "And I'm nowhere near ready."

Chapter Three

Eloise knew she ought to lash out indignantly at that arrogant pronouncement. Instead, when he put an arm around her waist and steered her toward the bed, she found herself following him without a moment's hesitation. Somehow she was sitting beside him on the edge of the mattress rather than shoving him into the hall. *Weird,* she thought. Not only her own behavior, but his. *I've heard of the casting couch for actresses, but never for writers!*

"I'm thirsty now," he said. "For your lips." He nibbled the edge of her mouth, darted his tongue in and out, then withdrew to gaze into her eyes.

What a hokey B-movie line, she thought. Yet "thirsty" seemed a perfectly apt word for her own dry-mouthed, head-whirling excitement. Or possibly "fever." "We shouldn't—" she began.

"You desire this as much as I do. I wouldn't touch you

otherwise." His hand rested between her breasts. "I feel it in the beating of your heart."

She opened her mouth, whether to confess or deny, she wasn't sure. He cut off her answer with a deeper kiss. A taste and scent like hot metal flooded her senses. His tongue and lips seared hers while his hand on the curve of her breast sent electric currents through her, switching every erogenous zone to "on." The flutter in the pit of her stomach migrated lower and became a full-fledged throb of need.

Good thing he couldn't read her mind. He couldn't know how her nipples strained against her bra, begging for a caress, or how her clit tickled maddeningly and wetness pooled between her thighs. She crossed her legs and squeezed. With his fingers creeping under the V of her dress, the pressure didn't bring any relief.

As if he did read her mind, he abandoned that tactic and instead cupped her right breast through the satin. Rubbing in slow circles, he coaxed the nipple to a hard peak. The other one ached for the same attention. Instantly, Claude draped his free arm around her shoulder to reach her left breast and fondle both in the same rhythm. Meanwhile, his tongue continued to probe her mouth. She fought to keep from squirming. Without her conscious will, she unfastened the top buttons of his shirt and ran her fingers over his chest. No undershirt, just cool skin and velvety hair. With the fog of lust clouding her brain, she gave no more than a fleeting thought to the difference from the usual texture of male body hair.

"You'll be more comfortable lying down," he murmured, nuzzling her neck. She felt him grope behind her to unzip her dress.

This would be the proper moment to cut the encounter

short. Never in her life had she fallen into bed with a man on first meeting. Claude's erotic expertise and her crush on him shouldn't matter. Contaminating business with sex, losing her self-respect and, for all she knew, risking some ghastly disease would be far worse than a few minutes of frustration. Besides, she could remedy that frustration by herself as soon as he left.

Before she realized she had moved, though, she lay on her back, with Claude reclining on one elbow next to her. He captured her mouth for another long kiss while he slid the dress off her shoulders. His practiced skill at undoing the front clasp of her bra stung her with a pang of jealousy. How many women did he seduce per year? Probably one at every convention.

She forgot that question the moment his tongue traced a path to one breast and spiraled inward to the peak. After slipping off her bra, he licked that nipple while teasing the other with thumb and forefinger. Somehow he knew just the pressure and speed to send ripples of pleasure through every nerve.

Involuntarily, she clutched his shoulders and eased her thighs apart. One of his legs covered hers with tantalizing pressure against her slit through her skirt. Already she trembled on the edge of orgasm. He abandoned the nipple for a brief, hard kiss on her mouth. "You taste as delicious as I expected." Passion roughened his voice, lending the words a tone of sincerity she hadn't anticipated.

He probably uses that line on all his victims. By now it didn't matter though. Her clit and her vagina ached for relief. And hearing the same need in his voice, she couldn't deny him.

She arched her hips, trying to press her swollen clit against his leg. He moved aside, drawing a hiss of protest from her. Removing her shoes and reaching under her skirt, he swept his palm up the inside of her calf and thigh. On this summer evening, she hadn't worn pantyhose. Her bare skin tingled, making her tremble with impatience for him to reach her hot, wet center. He cupped her mound through the bikini panties, silencing her moan of pleasure with a kiss.

Fumbling inside his shirt, she dug her nails into his chest. He growled and nibbled a path from her mouth to her neck. At the same time, he stretched the elastic of the panties to part her petals and caress the throbbing bud. Her clit started to twitch the instant he touched it. The frenzied licking of his tongue at her throat matched the rapid strokes of his fingers. When the throbbing began deep inside, he plunged two fingers into her slit while his thumb kept rubbing the spot that ached most desperately.

She erupted like that volcano they had mentioned earlier, pumping her hips in time with his finger-thrusts. When she hit the peak and began to spiral down, he nipped her neck and flicked her clit in some magical way that sent her even higher.

At last, soaring to a height so rarefied it sucked the breath from her lungs, she fell off the precipice into oblivion.

Chapter Four

When she opened her eyes, a rosy mist clouded her vision, and her throat felt dry. After dragging herself to a sitting position, she rubbed her face and looked around. *Oh, Lord, I can't believe I acted that way! How can I ever face Claude again?*

Come to think of it, where was he? His cape still hung over the chair, but he was nowhere to be seen, and she didn't hear any sounds from the bathroom. No way could she look him in the eye, at least not until she'd put some distance between herself and her humiliating cat-in-heat behavior. Maybe he'd be gentleman enough, next time they met, to pretend the encounter had never happened. Meanwhile, she had to get out before he reappeared. When he saw her gone, with luck he would return to his own room and leave her alone.

Standing up, she had to grab the bedpost until a

surge of dizziness faded. Noticing how loosely the bodice of her dress hung, she reached behind and pulled up the zipper. Muzzy-headed, she staggered out the door and along the hall to the elevator, one hand on the wall for balance. By the time she'd ridden to the ground floor, the danger of toppling over at every step had passed. Her brain still felt like oatmeal though. She drifted through the lobby to the main doors, with a vague idea of letting the night air clear her head.

She shoved through the double glass doors and meandered to the corner of Wilshire Boulevard.

Claude came back from his foray to the vending machines with a full ice bucket and a can of Coke. After her involuntary donation, Eloise would feel dehydrated. Even before unlocking the room door, he sensed her absence. What the devil had got into the woman? He hadn't expected her to wake so quickly, but what had possessed her to run off the moment she did?

And without her shoes, he noticed. Or her key, which he'd taken with him. While these thoughts ran through his mind, he was already heading for the stairs. He could dash to street level on his own power faster than the elevator could arrive and carry him down. If Eloise hadn't gone all the way to the first floor, he could search the hotel at leisure. The first priority was intercepting her if she was indeed wandering around the lobby barefoot and half-conscious. Damn, this was the last thing he wanted to be doing after the mutually satisfying "dessert" they'd sampled.

Hurrying from the stairwell into the lobby, he scanned the area. Just in time, he caught a glimpse of Eloise disappearing out the main entrance. He strode after her as fast as possible without breaking into a trot. She paused at the corner. As he walked toward her, he noticed the dreamy vagueness of her gaze. She stepped off the curb with no sign of noticing the red stoplight. Claude darted into the stream of traffic, wrapped his arms around her and flashed back to the sidewalk too fast for human eyes to follow.

Clinging to him, she shook her head in obvious bewilderment. "Claude——?"

He sensed the fog lifting from her brain. In a second she would start complaining about the way he'd chased and grabbed her. He also sensed eyes boring into him. Not just the curious glances of people who wondered how a man in a tuxedo and a barefoot woman in a formal gown had suddenly appeared on the sidewalk. Hostile eyes that felt not quite human.

He wasted no time processing this impression. Choosing action over analysis, he draped himself in a psychic veil that repelled vision. He projected a "you don't see me" aura that amounted to invisibility. With Eloise held close to him, she fell under the same curtain. Casual passersby would blink at their "disappearance" then instantly forget about them. As for the watcher who troubled Claude the most, if he, she or it existed at all, the illusion might provide enough time for an unseen retreat to the shelter of Eloise's room.

As she murmured confused protests, Claude carried her up the stairs to that refuge. "What the blazes is wrong with you?" he said as he plopped her on the bed. "Where did you think you were going?" And why did his own heart hammer with alarm at her narrow escape? He tabled that question for the moment.

"Out, if it's any of your business." Her flushed cheeks stirred his appetite even though he'd just feasted on her.

"It's my business when you nearly get yourself killed. What the devil did you want to run away for? Surely I didn't do anything to frighten you, did I?" He smoothed the hair straggling out of her braid.

She jerked her head away from his hand. "Of course not. I just wanted to be alone."

"Really?" He captured her eyes with his.

"If you must know, I was embarrassed." She gasped at her own frankness. He knew she must feel baffled by the way the truth had popped out.

Maintaining the gentle pressure of his mind on hers, he prompted, "Why in the world would you be embarrassed?"

"Humiliated. The way I acted when you, you know, touched me." The heat radiating from her skin made him want to absorb every drop of her essence.

"I enjoyed every minute of it. And so did you, didn't you?" He stroked her head, and this time she didn't resist. His hypnotic gaze and touch already had her partly tamed. "Here, you're thirsty," he said. He held the cold soda can to her mouth. She drank half of it and licked her lips in a maddeningly sensual way. He held her close and crooned a wordless song of languid pleasure until she went limp in his arms. "Don't worry about it. Lie down and rest. Everything is all right now."

He lowered her head onto the pillow and turned her on her side to unzip her dress. After peeling it off, he folded back the covers and tucked her in with the sheet up to her waist. He knew he ought to leave now, but her half-closed eyes watched him with drowsy lust that sparked a burning in the pit of his stomach.

Damn, I want her again! I can't remember the last time I was this hungry for a donor! If he couldn't remember, he told himself with an ironic smile, maybe the answer was "never." In any case, resisting temptation had never been his forte. Earlier, he could have satisfied his thirst without bringing her to climax. Her arousal alone would have spiced her blood. Her eagerness, though, had inflamed him past caution. Now the sight of her bare breasts, flushed with passion, and the aroma of her female musk, tinged with traces of soap and bath powder, overcame the remnants of his scruples. After all, what harm would another sip do?

Turning down the sheet, he scanned her aura, rose-tinted with desire. The blood humming just below the surface of her skin radiated heat, denser at her lips, the tips of her breasts and the triangle between her legs. He kissed her while his fingers skimmed over her breast and abdomen, to the center from which the fragrance of her arousal emanated. With splayed hands he swept down her body, up again, over and over. Her excitement coursed along the path of his caresses to thicken and pool at her core. Rainbows of scarlet, magenta and gold whirled in her aura. He stretched the elastic of her panties to probe her wetness. Her wiggle of pleasure almost goaded him into biting her at once. Clamping down on the impulse, he paused to slip off her panties.

Sighing, she wrapped her arms around his neck. His jaws ached, the roots of his teeth tingled and saliva flooded his mouth. At the same time, her emotions and sensations swirled around him. He felt the mild confusion underlying her excitement and smoothed her forehead to erase that perplexity before suckling her nipples and stroking the damp curls on her mound to stir her appetite afresh. Her legs eased apart, and she murmured wordless sounds of impatience. Licking the curve of her neck to prepare it for his teeth, he tasted salt and talcum. He felt the taut straining of her breast in his hand, the peak tantalizing the sensitive hairs in his palm. He felt the growing heat and tension spread from that point to the apex of her thighs. The air that enveloped them thrummed with the echo of her heartbeat.

He couldn't wait any longer. He nipped her throat with the razor-edge of his incisors, drawing a hot, tangy-sweet trickle of blood. The frenzied lapping of his tongue made her groan aloud, clutching his shoulders and pressing her heels into the mattress. Her urgency hammered at his consciousness. Exploring her secret places until he felt her excitement reach its highest pitch, he invaded her slit and simultaneously strummed the tight bud nestled in the curls. A keening cry burst from her. Her sheath clenched around his fingers. Flavored with her ecstasy, her blood rushed to his head like sparkling wine.

More than food, more than a sweet, intoxicating liqueur, her elixir ignited a miniature starburst in every cell of his body. He sometimes felt sorry for his prey, who experienced fulfillment only as a brief, localized spasm in the genitals. When he shared Eloise's climax, it flooded his entire being and went on and on, as long as his need demanded.

He goaded her to convulsions of delirium again and again. Finally, when both of them trembled with exhaustion, he blotted the tiny incision with a tissue until it stopped bleeding. "Sleep now," he murmured, stroking her hair. She relaxed onto the pillow with a long sigh, her eyes closing. "The wound will heal quickly. You won't even notice it. Forget the details of this night. Just remember that we shared pleasure. I'll see you soon." He kissed her forehead.

Soon. Their next meeting couldn't happen soon enough for him. If she responded this passionately in a mesmerized trance, how would she react if he took her in full awareness? *That way lies madness, old thing.* Plenty of women relished the fantasy of a vampire's kiss. More often than not, forcing them to accept the fantasy as real meant disaster.

Chapter Five

Eloise awoke dizzy and dry-mouthed, with sunlight beating on her eyes. Why hadn't she closed the curtains the night before? Come to think of it, she didn't exactly remember going to bed. What was the last thing she remembered? Staggering to the bathroom sometime in the wee hours.

Okay, not very useful information. Before that? Blinking as her eyes adjusted to daylight, she flipped back the covers. She was naked. *Oh, Lord, did Claude undress me and put me to bed?* Why couldn't she recall any details? Only a muddled impression of lips and hands exploring her most tender places, followed by multiple explosions in a spot that tingled at the mere thought.

Yet she knew no penetration had occurred. In fact, from what few images she could retrieve, Claude hadn't even taken his pants off. So what did he get out of reducing her to a puddle of molten lava?

She rolled over and buried her face in the pillow with a groan. And this was the man she expected to work with on the project that would save her from losing her home? She'd probably swoon the moment she met his eyes, like one of the fainting heroines in her script.

The script. Had he meant everything he'd said, or had the whole conversation been a ploy to get her clothes off? At that thought, her attention strayed to the way the sheet felt on her bare skin. Vague memories of where his fingers had roamed woke a deep ache inside her. She tucked the spare pillow between her legs and rocked, suddenly overwhelmed by sensory echoes of Claude's cool touch and flickering tongue. The ache blossomed into shudders of release.

She lay panting and trembling until her breath slowed to normal. *What's he done to me?* Thrusting the pillow aside, she sat up and surveyed the room. Claude's cape and bow tie had disappeared. In place of the synopsis and partial, a business card and a sheet of hotel stationery lay on the desk. She put on her reading glasses and skimmed the note: "Thank you for a delightful evening. I'll get in touch with you this week to discuss details of our *Varney* adaptation. Meanwhile, if anything happens that requires immediate attention, call one of the numbers on my card."

Delightful evening? Yeah, she could endorse that description, but she'd have been much more delighted if she could have remembered exactly what she'd done. She hadn't imbibed enough wine to get blackout-level drunk, and Claude couldn't have found a chance to drug her drink, even if he'd have reason to do such a ridiculous thing. Immediate attention? *Oh, wow, I'd love some more of that attention!*

She mentally gave herself a sound shaking and headed for

the shower. Next time she met Claude, she'd keep the encounter all business

Home in Pasadena on Monday, Eloise focused on work—the novel she had assigned herself as her summer's project. There didn't seem any reason to compose more of the *Varney* script until she'd discussed it further with Claude, to whom she didn't devote a minute's thought after leaving the convention. No more than a minute each hour of the day, anyhow.

About nine on Monday evening, sitting at the computer in her home office, she answered the phone and heard an unfamiliar male voice. When he began, "Miss Eloise Kern?" she pigeonholed him as a telemarketer. Who else would speak her full name in that tentative tone?

Preoccupied with nothing worse than irritation over his calling so late, she got an unpleasant jolt when he said, "I saw you at the hotel on Saturday with Claude Darvell. Do you intend to associate with him further?" The stiffly formal phrases in a quiet, cultured voice clashed oddly with the boldness of the question.

"Why do you ask, and who the heck are you anyway?" Her pulse hammered in her ears.

"Someone who knows who and what Darvell actually is. That man is dangerous. For your own safety, stay away from him."

"What do you mean, dangerous? Talk sense or leave me alone!" She heard a tremor in her own voice. She wasn't sure whether the fear seeping into her veins was directed at this anonymous caller or at Claude.

"If I explained, you would not believe me. But I know him well, and I am warning you against him. He is a killer."

"Look here, you—"

The man hung up.

After her breathing steadied, she got out Claude's business card and picked up the phone again.

Claude's surprised pleasure at hearing Eloise's voice turned to alarm when she explained the situation.

"I just got an anonymous phone call from some strange man warning me to stay away from you." The words tumbled out, high-pitched with anxiety.

"Did he say why?"

"No, just that you're dangerous. Do you know who he is?"

"I have an idea." *Philip! Damn it, how did he find her?*

"Are you being stalked by a crazy fan, or what?"

"Something of the sort."

"Well, what's he bothering me for?" Her tone sounded accusatory, and no wonder.

"Never mind that. The important thing is to keep you safe. I'm on my way over."

"You're what?"

"I'm leaving for your place right now. Stay inside and don't answer the door until I get there." He wished he could exert his will on her over the phone. The best he could do was to inject a decisive tone into the order.

"Claude, I don't know what you think you're doing, but aren't you overreacting?"

"No. You didn't think so when you called me, *n'est-ce pas?* Now, will you do as I ask?"

"Oh, all right, but when you get here, you better bring some straight answers."

Throughout the twenty-minute drive to Pasadena, Claude fumed at the traffic. Too bad his limited power of shape-shift-

ing and levitation didn't enable him to fly the sixteen miles
and avoid the mess. On the other hand, if he changed into a
bat like his movie counterparts, he would arrive at Eloise's
without a car, which he needed to get her out of Philip's reach.
On reflection, it seemed obvious that, despite Claude's efforts,
Philip had noticed him with Eloise. The other vampire would
then have easily discovered her name and address by hypnotizing a hotel clerk. Claude realized he'd counted too heavily on
Philip's unfamiliarity with this time and place. Apparently the
man had made efficient use of the month since his revival.

Once off the freeway in Pasadena, Claude had no trouble
finding Eloise's townhouse from the map he'd memorized.
Instead of stopping, he drove two blocks farther, parked and
walked back. He shrouded himself in a psychic veil to deflect
any watcher's vision. At the door he rang the bell and heard
Eloise's footsteps approaching.

The sound of her rapid, shallow breaths reached him
through the wooden panel, along with the rattle of the chain
being unhooked. He cursed under his breath at her lack of
caution. At the last second, though, she remembered to ask,
"Who's there?"

He gave his name, holding the illusion of invisibility until
the door opened. He slipped inside, then closed and latched
it behind him. Eloise looked up at him, eyes wide and lips
parted. Her aura quivered with anxiety echoed in the racing
of her pulse.

"Has he called again?" said Claude.

She shook her head. "What's the idea of scaring me half to
death? And what are you doing here anyway?"

"What, not glad to see me?" Before she had time to object,
he wrapped his arms around her. She leaned her head on his
chest. He smoothed her unbound hair until her strong, young

heart slowed to a steady beat. "It's all right, *chérie*. I won't let him near you."

Sighing, she pushed away from him. He let her go. "Who is this guy, and why should I be afraid of him? He claims you're a killer. What does that mean? You owe me an explanation."

He followed her from the entryway into the living room, furnished with a wing-backed couch, two matching chairs and floor-to-ceiling bookshelves. "It's too complicated to explain. I can tell you that he's a former friend who thinks he has a legitimate grudge against me, and he'll take it out on you if he can. But I can assure you I haven't killed anyone." He reinforced the last sentence with a psychic nudge. True enough, he hadn't murdered Philip's woman, although he could understand why Philip saw it that way.

Standing in the middle of the room with her arms folded, Eloise glared at him. "Yeah? Why me? You and I just met."

"Ah, but he doesn't know that. He must have seen us together at the convention, noticed that I spent several hours in your room—"

She blushed. "And somehow got my name from the hotel staff. Okay, I get the picture. That doesn't explain why you rushed over here."

"To take you to safety, of course. We're going to my house on Big Sur."

"What you mean 'we,' white man?" she quoted the old Tonto joke. "You hit the freeway back to Beverly Hills. I'm not going anywhere."

He closed the distance between them in two strides, prepared to grab her if she decided to stalk out of the room. "Do you have any obligations that would make it impossible for you to leave for a few days?"

"No, I'm not teaching a class this summer, but that's

beside the point. I didn't ask you to show up and whisk me away on your white horse."

"Actually, it's a dark blue Mercedes." His lips quirked in an involuntary smile at the indignation sparking from her. "This man knows where you live. I simply want to take you somewhere, temporarily, where he can't find you."

"You haven't given me a good reason to dive down a rabbit hole. And even if you had, I can take care of myself."

"Not against this threat, you can't, damn it." He caught her by the upper arms, just below the short sleeves of the clinging T-shirt she wore. *Oh, hell, trying to be patient with ephemerals never gets me very far anyway.* He captured her eyes and gave her a gentle psychic nudge. "You'll be safer with me. Let me protect you."

Her folded arms and clenched fists relaxed, and the resistance melted out of her. "Protect me? Okay. I'll be safer with you."

"That's right. You'll be safe in my house up the coast."

"Uh-huh." Wrapping her arms loosely around his waist, she leaned on him again. "Safe."

The heat of her flesh and the throbbing of her pulse tempted him to put off their departure long enough for a kiss or two, if not a quick nibble. The trusting way she snuggled up to his chest made his throat go dry, even though he'd implanted that trust himself. But this was no time for dalliance. For all he knew, Philip might be watching the house.

With a murmur of regret, Claude pushed Eloise to arm's length and gazed into her eyes again. "Go pack whatever you'll need. And you may as well bring your *Varney* materials. We can work on the thing while we're down the rabbit hole."

The last remark penetrated her daze enough to evoke a vague smile. He paced the room, ears pricked for any sound of a third person lurking outside, until she reappeared with an overnight bag, briefcase and purse. He noticed that part of the fog he'd imposed on her brain had evaporated.

"Claude, where are we going again, and why?"

Staring into her eyes, he said with all the firmness he could muster, "We're going to my other home, about three hundred miles up the coast, where you'll be safe. Take my word for it and don't worry."

Her eyelids drooped. "Okay, not worried."

"Wait a second." He moved to the window and peered out between the curtains. No sign of Philip. Not that there would be, if the stalker had psychically cloaked himself. Hesitating for that reason would accomplish nothing.

Claude put an arm around Eloise to hold her as close as possible while they walked out the door. He rebuilt his shield of illusion, extending it to cover her too. As long as she stayed in physical contact with him and didn't do anything to attract attention, both of them should remain "invisible."

"What are you doing?" she murmured, locking the door on the way out.

"Nothing you need to worry about. Just walk with me quietly."

They made the two-block trip to the car without incident. Claude only hoped Philip wasn't lurking unseen along the way. After stowing Eloise's things in the back seat, Claude belted her into the passenger seat up front and gave her another order to relax. "You probably need rest. Why don't you take a nap?"

Immediately, her head slumped, and her eyes closed. *Good, I haven't lost the touch.* It was a wonder his own anxiety hadn't kept hers alive. His barely leashed fear for her baffled him. Why did he suddenly care so much about an ephemeral's welfare? Mentally shaking off the question, he started the car and headed westward to the coast.

Chapter Six

er neck felt stiff, her eyes gritty. Bewildered to find herself in a moving car, Eloise looked around with a momentary heart-stutter of panic. When she saw Claude in the driver's seat, the fear subsided. He wasn't scary, just overbearing and infuriating. She rubbed her face. "Where are we?"

He glanced over at her. "On Highway One, north of L.A., on our way to Big Sur."

"But why—" A second later, the evening's events came back to her. "Oh, yeah, you talked me into skipping town with you. How on earth did you do that?"

He shrugged. "No doubt you recognized the irresistible logic of my argument."

"The one where you claimed some guy is stalking both of us, but you wouldn't tell me why? That argument?"

He just flashed her a smile.

"And you still won't tell me? Oh, I give up!" She

stretched her legs, bemused to notice that she'd left home in the middle of the night in shorts, a T-shirt and sandals. "I hope you realize I can't make a three-hundred-mile trip without stopping."

"Of course. I trust you won't run away though."

"Where to? You think I'd try to hitchhike back to Pasadena? No, I'll stick with you, even if you did kidnap me."

He laughed. "'The highwayman came riding, riding, up to the old inn door.'"

Recognizing the poem, she retorted, "Don't expect me to make with the sappy devotion like Bess, the landlord's daughter."

At the next roadside convenience stop, he pulled in to fuel the car. After using the facilities, Eloise bought a bottle of water and a handful of snacks. It crossed her mind that it would serve him right if she did disappear, but caution prevailed.

Back on the road, he said, "You don't happen to have a dashing highwayman who'll ride to your rescue, by the way? I mean, a fiancé or the equivalent who'll challenge me to pistols at dawn because of our temporary elopement?"

She blushed at that word. If she had to elope with anyone, Claude would rank high on the list. "No, not since graduate school." She'd broken up with her last fiancé-equivalent when he'd taken his domineering behavior one step too far. She'd recognized his true character when he'd announced to her that they were going to get married and move to New Jersey, where he'd accepted a job, instead of consulting her first. Claude, at least, was only kidnapping her as far as central California. By the scenic route, no less. Of course, she would have been able to enjoy the oceanfront scenery better if it hadn't been the middle of the night.

"I didn't know you had a house up the coast," she said.

"I try not to let it get around. My official bio mentions the penthouse in Los Angeles, the townhouse in London and the chalet on Lake Geneva. Since this other place doesn't get publicized, I'm hoping the man who called you won't know it exists."

"You really are rich, aren't you?" She blushed deeper, wondering why his presence made her blurt out such things. "I mean, I can't help asking why you bother to work. You must love acting."

"Yes, and I find the human contact—stimulating."

Eloise shivered. How did that one word spark such vivid memories of the sensations he'd incited in her Saturday night? She stared out her window, glad he couldn't possibly see her flushed cheeks in the dark. "It's just hard for me to imagine having four houses. I'm having enough trouble hanging onto one."

"What do you mean?"

She told him about her problem with the condo conversion. "I really want to buy the townhouse. I planned to all along, but I didn't think it would happen so fast. If I can't swing the mortgage, I'll have to look for a new place, and you know L.A. real estate prices. I shudder to think how hard it'll be to find another decent rental I can afford."

"The down payment is the snag, then?"

"Yes, it's taking a while to save up, with my mother's nursing home fees and all." At his questioning glance, she said, "Alzheimer's. My dad died years ago, and I'm an only child, so it's all on me."

"Can you not borrow the balance of the down payment?"

The rich really did live in a different world. "It'll be enough trouble getting approved for the mortgage. Do you have any idea how loan officers react to the word 'writer' on the 'occupation' line? They see it as equivalent to 'unemployed.' Sure, I have my teaching income, but that's part-time. If I took a full-time faculty post, I wouldn't be able to keep producing two novels a year."

"I see your quandary," he said. "But I sense the townhouse means more to you than an investment."

How did he know? "My father was a career officer in the Navy. We never owned a house until he retired to San Diego. Then he died of a heart attack before he had time to enjoy it. And when Mom went into full-time care, we had to sell the place. So a home of my own has been my dream for a long time."

"Then the *Varney* project has special importance for you."

"Yes, and now I've bored you with all my problems," she said, embarrassed at having complained about her financial bind to a man she hardly knew. "So it's your turn to spill secrets."

"What secrets? You've read the publicity bio."

"Which doesn't mention a lot besides the three houses, your Anglo-French background and the fact that acting runs in your family."

"That's all there is to tell, essentially. I've led a fairly dull life, for which I'm thankful. You know the curse about interesting times."

The official biography didn't even reveal where his money came from. "Inherited wealth" didn't say much. The list of his movies stretched back over twenty years, raising the question of his age at the start of his career. He looked just barely old enough to make the dates plausible, and the bio was frustratingly short of specifics for the early period. As for the continental side of his lineage, except for the occasional French phrase that spiced his conversation, he spoke with a thoroughly British accent. The bio said he'd been born in France but had spent most of his life in England.

Obviously, questioning him wouldn't pry loose any information. Eloise decided to rest and enjoy what she could see of the view.

After five hours, including two more rest stops, the car wound along the stretch of road high above the Big Sur coastline. Though she still couldn't see much in the dark, she heard the waves through Claude's open window when he slowed down and turned off the highway down a narrow lane that led toward the shore. A private drive, she realized when he pulled to a stop in front of what looked like a two-story house. Getting out, she saw it from a different angle that revealed a third, lower floor, split-level style, in back. Gnarled cypress trees shaped by ocean winds huddled next to the house. Motion sensors switched on floodlights to illuminate the carport and front door. She caught an impression of redwood siding and sloping roofs before Claude escorted her inside.

"'Enter freely and of your own will,'" he said as he waved her into the foyer.

"Thanks, Count," she said, acknowledging the quote from *Dracula.* "I hope you don't have dungeons and a crypt. Not to mention a harem of lady vampires."

His hand rested lightly on her back, making her shiver with pleasure out of proportion to the casualness of the contact. "Why would I need a harem with you under my roof?" He steered her toward a staircase but then broke off the touch.

Feeling mildly let down, she followed him to the top floor.

There he showed her to a corner bedroom with a door opening onto a balcony. The other outside wall held a window with a double bed under it. Claude strode over to the door and opened it to let in the salt-flavored breeze and the sound of the waves. "It should be safe enough to leave this open, if you like."

"Why shouldn't it be? Do you think your former friend, or whatever he is, would fly in the window like a bat?" She walked over to the balcony to look out. Aside from a streak of moonlight on the water, she couldn't see anything. "No street lights, no neon signs, just the night. It's beautiful—but strange. To me, anyway."

He placed his hand in the middle of her back then skimmed down to her waistline. "I'm delighted to have a chance to share it with you." He reached under the hem of her shirt to stroke the bare skin at the small of her back.

Stifling a gasp at the coolness of his touch, she turned toward him. His other hand reached up to smooth her hair, lingering at her temple where the pulse throbbed. His fingers, almost chill in contrast to her own flushed face, felt refreshing. So how could that coolness ignite such a fire at her core?

He leaned toward her, nuzzled her hair, kissed her forehead. And stopped. Instead of tracing a path to her parted lips, he straightened up. No longer touching, he stepped away from her. "You must be exhausted after being kidnapped." An ironic smile punctuated the sentence. "Sleep as long as you want." He retreated so fast she could almost imagine being near her made him nervous.

Which made no sense, considering his behavior on their first meeting. Unless the excitement vibrating through her body was contagious.

Nevertheless, by the time she finished taking a hot shower

in the bathroom next door, her tension drained into utter weariness. She fell asleep minutes after crawling into bed.

Claude lurked in the hall outside Eloise's room, listening to her breathing slow to the rhythm of sleep. The last thing he should do was invade her dreams with his hunger. He'd brought her here partly for protection and partly for work on the script, not to serve as his live-in buffet. Yet her avid response was so hard to resist. Not only did her body open lavishly to his touch, so did her mind. He recalled how freely she had poured out her problems in their conversation. The down payment she fretted about would, he knew, amount to pocket change for him. Anyone who survived for centuries could accumulate a comfortable fortune as long as he didn't make himself a target by flaunting it. Claude knew there was no use offering money to Eloise though. She wouldn't accept a gift or even a loan.

All the more reason to focus on the movie project, to give him a legitimate pretext for handing her the solution to her financial woes. Besides, repeatedly feeding on her could expose her to greater danger from Philip. Claude's mark on her aura would make it plain that she meant more to him than a casual donor. If Philip wanted revenge for the loss he'd suffered so many decades before, he would leap at the chance to prey on Claude's pet.

Not that he planned to make a pet of Eloise. Yet the drumbeat of her heart, audible through the closed door, drew him like a moth to flame. Except that his appetite was the flame that might consume her. Even while he rehashed the arguments against tasting her again, he opened the door, slipped inside and glided to the bed.

Well, I never claimed to have a conscience. He sat on the edge of the mattress, spreading a net of hypnotic influence to keep her from waking at the disturbance. With a sigh, she turned in her sleep. The sheet slid an inch to reveal the curve of a breast. She wore a low-cut, satin nightgown. When Claude traced a line from the hollow of her throat to the V between her breasts, her pulse accelerated. He felt the blood rushing through her heart under his open hand. The tiny hairs in his palm bristled with eagerness to stroke every inch of her smooth, warm flesh.

With his other hand, he turned down the covers. The nightgown was tangled around her hips. He skimmed up one exposed thigh and down the inside of the other. Her lips parted to emit a soft moan.

He kissed her forehead, jaw line, throat, the pulse fluttering against his lips like that moth he'd visualized, now trapped in a spider's web. "This is a dream, *ma belle*," he whispered. "Only a dream. Embrace me."

Her arms twined around his neck. Licking and nibbling her throat and the curve of her breast, teasing both her and himself without piercing the skin, he ran his hands over her body, barely touching, stirring the hues of her aura into whirlpools of rose and crimson. Her nipples and mound of Venus, engorged with blood, glowed like clusters of painless sunlight.

Ravenous from the aroma of the sweet nectar between her legs and her excitement sparking like miniature stars everywhere he caressed her, he chased that excitement to its source and tickled the taut nubbin of flesh that begged for his attention. Her hips undulated while she clung to him and moaned her pleasure, although her conscious mind still slept.

"Open to me," he murmured. Not a moth, he thought,

but a bee ready to drink her honey. He would never let his
sting cause her pain though.

Her thighs parted. He dipped a finger in her dewy center
and stroked her throbbing bud. Throwing her head back on
the pillow, she arched her spine and keened in ecstasy. Her
heart hammered in time with the pulsation of her climax.

At the instant that her release would imbue her blood with
the sweetest flavor, he nipped the swell of her breast. With the
trickle of blood, her passion fountained forth, as intoxicating
as strong mead.

His teeth-roots ached too badly for gentle licking to satisfy him. He fastened onto her breast and sucked hard. Her
elixir flooded his parched throat and suffused every cell of his
body. When he strummed her most sensitive spot again, her
second climax shot through him like a bolt of lightning.

If only he could keep her forever, not as a pet, but as
something more. How would it feel if she opened her eyes
and her mind, recognized his true nature and still welcomed
him into her embrace? He yearned to warm himself at the
flame of her innermost core. Realizing the folly of that wish,
he longed to spend the rest of this night, at least, sipping her
sweet nectar. But he forced himself to listen to the voice of
moderation.

After the long night's drive and the self-indulgent way
he'd behaved at the convention only a couple of nights earlier, he knew she needed rest. He reluctantly forced himself
to remove his mouth from the incision and calm her with languid petting, rather than goading her to fresh excitement.

"Remember, my dear," he said as he straightened her
nightgown and covered her with the sheet, "this was only a
dream."

Life would be simpler if he could delude himself into believing the same thing.

A cool wind swept in through the open balcony door. Thunder cleaved the night. In a flash of lightning, Eloise saw a tall man in a black cape silhouetted in the portal. At the neck of his ruffled, white shirt, he wore a ruby pin like a globule of fresh blood.

When he strode toward her bed, she recognized Claude.

At that point she realized she was dreaming. She decided that was all right. In a dream she could indulge any craving without fear of consequences. She opened her arms, and Claude swooped down upon her.

His hot mouth feasted on her lips, her neck, her breasts. Somehow their clothes dissolved. His hands roamed over her bare skin. She felt his tongue bathing both nipples, then flickering down her abdomen to her mound, where he probed inside the nest of hair for the sheltered nub of flesh. His tongue tip found the flashpoint of her need, quicker than she could have herself. She screamed aloud when the convulsion ripped through her.

Then he licked his way up to her neck and lay on top of her to press his leg between hers, in the place that still burned and tingled. Her tight nipples strained against his naked chest. She felt a sting at her throat, followed by a thread of hot liquid and the lapping of his tongue. He groaned with pleasure, and her voice joined his. She wrapped her legs around his thigh and squeezed. Delicious melting sensations flowed from her throat through her quivering nerves to that hot center. She shuddered in release until exhaustion overcame her.

When Claude sat up, another flash of lightning showed

dark stains around his mouth. Licking his lips clean, he pulled up the covers over her. "Sleep, my dear, and remember this was only a dream."

"Yes, I know," she murmured as he faded into mist. Only in a dream could she imagine Claude to be a real vampire instead of an actor who sometimes played one.

Chapter Seven

irds chirping outside the window woke her. With her eyes still shut, Eloise listened to the other noise in the background, waves on a beach. A cool breeze drifted across her face, carrying the aroma of salt water. What was she doing beside the ocean?

She opened her eyes. Sunlight streamed in through a door that opened onto a balcony. Oh, right, Claude's Big Sur waterfront house. He'd kidnapped her. Well, as kidnappers' lairs went, she could enjoy this one. Especially if the sea air always inspired dreams like the one she'd had the night before. Feeling warmth flood her whole body, she hurried to the bathroom next door for a cool shower. If she expected to make a movie deal with Claude, she had to get a grip and act like a professional writer, not a swooning fan with a mad crush.

After dressing in jeans and a lightweight, tunic-style

blouse and tying back her hair in a ponytail, she thought to check her watch. She'd slept until almost two in the afternoon. Her stomach reminded her that she'd also slept through breakfast and lunch. Still, curiosity demanded a quick tour of the house. The top floor, besides her bedroom and the bath, contained two other bedrooms, open and untenanted, and a closed door at the opposite end of the hall from her room. The absence of any sounds of life suggested Claude was asleep behind that door.

Stairs led to the main floor where they'd entered the previous night. Jokes aside, the place didn't look like a haunted castle. The foyer opened into a sunken living room with wall-to-wall carpet, a fireplace and an elaborate stereo system. Across the hall was an office. Despite her hunger, she couldn't resist pausing to examine the vintage movie posters and old photographs on the wall behind the desk, obviously part of Claude's family history.

One black-and-white poster advertised a film adaptation of *The Sorrows of Satan*, from a lurid early-twentieth-century novel. The star bore a striking resemblance to Claude, allowing for the devilish eyebrows and other exaggerations of the illustrator's style. His grandfather, or would it have to be great-grandfather? She'd never heard of the movie; it must be one of many silent films that hadn't survived. Photos from the 1940s era showed group poses that featured a man with a widow's-peak haircut and a pencil-thin mustache, doubtless Claude's father or uncle. She made a mental note to ask him, but now she had to scrounge some food before she keeled over from starvation.

Toward the back of the house she found the dining room and kitchen, which looked as clean as a model home in a very expensive housing development. The kitchen struck her as oddly empty, with nothing on the spacious counters except a blender and microwave and nothing on the walls, not even a rack of carving knives. The cooking island in the middle of the room displayed food at least. A box of granola and a bowl of apples didn't inspire gourmet fantasies, but her stomach decided they were better than nothing.

The refrigerator held milk, orange juice and nothing else. Rather than snooping in the freezer, she settled in the breakfast nook to gobble her cereal, apple and glass of juice. When she rinsed her dishes, she couldn't resist a peek in the cabinets. Other than the one where she had found the bowls and glasses, most of the cupboards were bare. Did Claude always live like Mother Hubbard? Or maybe he just didn't spend a lot of time in this house.

On the lowest level, she found a half-bath, a small sitting room with a wide-screen TV and a den with bookshelves lining all the walls except one, which featured sliding glass doors that opened onto a patio. She stepped outside, drawing a deep breath of the salty air. The house perched on the edge of a cliff above the shore. Wooden steps led from the patio down to the rock-strewn beach. The stony bluffs, too steep for walking or even comfortable climbing, formed a semicircle that completely enclosed what appeared to be Claude's private beachfront property. An effective way to ensure privacy, she mused.

Back inside, she still didn't hear any sign of life. She wandered into the TV room where she discovered a bookcase full of videotapes. Finding a Vincent Price collection on one shelf, she grabbed *The Fall of the House of Usher* and snuggled into an enormous armchair to watch the movie. Nothing was missing but the popcorn.

. . .

Just as the House of Usher started to topple into the lake, a touch on her shoulder jerked her out of the world on the screen. She turned with a gasp. "Good grief, Claude, warn me before you sneak up on me." She switched off the VCR.

"I am told I have a quiet footstep," he intoned in a Bela Lugosi accent.

"Too bad I don't have a mirror handy to test you with." Her pulse still raced from that momentary touch. She scanned his tall, greyhound-lean form, ravishing even in casual slacks and an open-necked polo shirt.

"Good, those secrets you asked about are still safe," he said. "I hope you found everything you needed. I apologize for the minimal breakfast selection, but I don't keep this place well stocked."

"That's okay." Following him up to the main floor, she said, "I love your house, and you have an incredible view from the patio."

"Wait until you see it at night. By the way, you didn't go outside, did you?" he asked as they entered the kitchen.

"Only for a second. What about it?"

"Please don't." He caught her arm and frowned. "Not without me."

His fingers felt like a brand on her skin. "Why on earth not? Come on, kidnapping is one thing, but I don't know if I can stand for house arrest."

"Confound it, I'm trying to protect you! Can't you take my word that I know what I'm talking about?"

She pulled away from him. "I would if you'd explain yourself." When he continued to glower at her, she said, "Oh, all right, I won't roam around outside by myself."

He visibly relaxed. "That's better. Now, you must be hungry. Again, I'm afraid my supplies are limited." He opened the freezer. "Would you prefer chicken, beef or fish?"

"Uh, chicken, I guess."

He confirmed her impression of him as a stereotypical bachelor non-cook by taking out a frozen fried chicken dinner and popping it in the microwave. While Eloise sat at the polished redwood table in the breakfast nook, Claude got a can of beef broth from one of the almost-empty cabinets and started it simmering on the stove. He then opened a bottle of cabernet and poured her a glass. "Here, have a drink. Have several."

"That's all you're eating?"

"I'm not hungry—now. Anyway, I suffer from a mind-boggling array of food allergies," he said, sitting opposite her with his own wineglass. "I survive mostly on a liquid protein diet."

"So you just keep the bare minimum of food around for visitors." That explained why the kitchen looked as if a famine had struck central California.

"Of which I don't have many here, as I said." He gazed at her over the rim of his glass. "I'm delighted to make you an exception."

Blushing under his intense scrutiny, she lowered her eyes to the table, glad the microwave interrupted the moment with a beep.

After he'd served her microwaved dinner and his mug of broth, he turned the conversation to the *Varney* plotline. "Now, about the opening scene. I leap out Flora's window, and her father and brother charge in pursuit and one of them shoots me, yes?"

"Right."

"Jolly good. In the book, the rays of the moon bring our Byronic bloodsucker back to life. Shall we use that?"

"Why not? It'll give the movie a fresh slant compared to all the other vampire films. In fact, I was thinking we should deliberately make it old-fashioned, just on the edge of camp but not quite."

"I like the way your mind works." He raised his glass to her. "So our baffled heroes search hither and yon, without finding a trace of the midnight intruder."

She smiled at the melodramatic flourish he gave to the words. "The next day, Varney shows up, the elegant gentleman who has just moved into town, offering to buy the mansion. So far, we're sticking to the plot of the book."

"Which we have to deviate from eventually, on account of those inconvenient eight hundred pages. Have you considered doing anything with the sexton who unearths the truth about Varney and blackmails him?" Claude delivered the "unearth" pun with a completely straight face.

"If we keep it simple. What if Varney spends the first night in his family crypt and the sexton catches him rising from the grave at sunset the next day?"

"Why doesn't Varney just kill the blighter?"

"Good question." Eloise stirred gravy around in her mashed potatoes. "The sexton fends him off with a cross, maybe? After all, they're in a churchyard."

With a thoughtful frown, Claude took a long drink from his mug of broth. "I suppose we're stuck with the bit about waving crosses in the vampire's face. Audiences expect it, and it's a convenient icon to brand him as a cursed creature of the night and all that." He emptied the cup and licked his lips.

Suppressing a shiver, she forced her eyes away from his

mouth. "Okay, he retires to his tomb, wakes up at sunset and gets into a confrontation with the sexton, then visits the Bannerworths and tries to charm them into selling the house. Oh, and somewhere along the way he has to move into rented quarters."

"Indeed." Claude refilled both of their wineglasses. "I always wonder about those vampires who live in mausoleums and still manage to have elegant wardrobes and perfect grooming." While pouring her wine, he leaned over her a few seconds longer than necessary. She felt his eyes linger on her long after he returned to his seat.

"That's as far as I've planned in any detail, except for the ending anyway." She picked at her fried chicken, trying to suppress her awareness of Claude's intense gaze. *He acts like my eating is the most fascinating spectacle he's seen all week.*

When she finished the meal, Claude suggested moving into the office. They brought the rest of the wine along. Eloise switched on the computer and inserted the disk she'd brought with her. "Do you have any ideas about the middle?" she asked, loading her file of unfinished plot notes. "Middles are always the hard part. Varney will try to seduce Flora, of course."

"Of course." Claude pulled up a chair beside the desk, so close that Eloise could feel his breath ruffling the fine hairs on her arms. His nostrils flared as if sampling her scent. "When I call on the Bannerworths, I pay particular attention to the innocent Flora. She doesn't recognize me, naturally."

"Sure, it has to work that way. You'll have to appear in heavy makeup, with huge fangs, in the first bedroom scene so the audience can believe she doesn't know it's you." She typed a note to that effect. "But she still feels uneasy. Something about you strikes a chord. I mean something about the vampire," she hastily corrected.

"Does it? What kind of chord?" He gave her a teasing half-smile.

"She's nervous but fascinated. It's a 'dove mesmerized by a snake' kind of thing." Feeling her face grow hot under his eyes, Eloise focused on the computer screen.

"And Varney knows exactly how she reacts, no matter how hard she tries to disguise it," said Claude, edging still closer. "He gloats over her fascination."

"How does he know?"

"What? Have you forgotten vampires can read emotions? He senses every feeling that flashes through her mind. He knows that underneath her fear, she craves his touch." He lowered his voice to a silken purr.

"He does, huh? Who made this rule about vampires reading emotions?" She flicked a brief glance at him then took a gulp of wine to distract herself from the new blush she felt creeping over her skin.

Claude shrugged. "Stands to reason. It goes along with their hypnotic power of mind control. They have to read it to control it, you know."

"Right." She forced a shaky giggle to deflect her own thoughts from the way he seemed able to creep into them and control them. "Mind control and emotion reading. Check." She typed the phrases. "No bat transformation, I hope? That's not in the book."

"Then let's skip it, by all means. He doesn't need wings to seduce Flora."

"Seduce? I thought he was trying to terrify her."

"Ah, but once he meets her in a less tumultuous situation, he changes his mind. Her wide, innocent eyes ensnare him." Claude captured Eloise's eyes, making her feel like a shard of metal in the grip of a magnet. "He can't resist the aroma of her blood and the liquid pulsation of her heart." His lips grazed her hair, and he inhaled as if savoring its aroma. He placed one finger on the hollow of her throat. "He lures her into his web under the very eyes of her father, brother and jealous suitor. He's determined to own the house and make her his bride as well."

Eloise felt her pulse throb under his fingertip. "But he doesn't," she said, forcing her voice to remain steady. "He doesn't possess Flora in the end."

"Quite right." Claude retreated to lean against the desk at arm's length from her. "According to your outline, you plan to use the double heroine device. The other girl, Clara, will be the expendable one."

She laughed, glad for the break in the tension. "That's such a crude way to put it. I'd rather think of Clara as the red shirt, like a *Star Trek* security guard."

"Varney turns to her as a consolation prize when Flora's family learns how to protect her from vampires," said Claude. "He's lonely for the embrace of a beautiful woman."

Eloise's skin prickled under his penetrating gaze. "Vampires get lonely?"

"Of course. The blood is the life, as they say. Not just food, but total fulfillment. When Flora rejects Varney, he needs a substitute."

She broke away from his stare and focused on the computer screen. "But he gets carried away with Clara—"

"And accidentally transforms her—"

"She rises from the grave and starts preying on the innocent—"

"So the vampire-hunting fanatics invade her resting place and drive a stake through her—"

"Which awakens Varney to the true horror of his existence. Realizing he'll never find peace, he decides to commit suicide in the crater of Vesuvius," Eloise finished.

"The graveyard scene should incorporate all the familiar details from the vintage vampire films. Torch-bearing peasants and the lot. The writhing undead corpse spouting fountains of blood."

"Sure, and vampire hunters loaded down with crosses, garlic and holy water."

Claude folded his arms and declaimed, "Garlic in a basket for the vampire in the casket, and a holy water flagon to keep her cape a-draggin'."

Eloise gave him an incredulous stare.

"I'll need a few minutes of rehearsal," he said, "if you want a better Danny Kaye parody than that. Holy water flask for the undead-splashing task?"

She shook her head. "You stick to performing the lines, and let somebody else write them."

Brandishing the wine bottle, he said, "Empty. Would you like some more?"

She finished typing her notes and stood up. She felt lightheaded and a little wobbly. "Maybe just one glass."

In the kitchen, she leaned against the center island and sliced an apple while he opened another bottle of wine. With the length of time that had passed since her not-so-filling dinner, maybe she needed some ballast in her stomach. The paring knife slipped and gashed her left thumb. Her arm jerked, banging her elbow on the counter. She yelped in pain.

Claude zipped over to her. "Are you all right? Let me see." He raised her hand to his lips and kissed the cut while he massaged her elbow. Instantly, warmth erased the pain in the joint, spread in concentric circles and radiated up her arm. She felt his tongue lick the wound before he started sucking it. The sting from the knife blade vanished, replaced by an electric tingle that made the skin prickle all over her body. Only half aware of what she was doing, she closed her eyes and leaned on Claude's chest.

He removed his mouth and stepped back, holding her hand lightly. Dismayed by the sudden interruption of the dreamy contentment that had enveloped her, she stared up at him.

"There, it's stopped bleeding," he said. His breathing sounded as labored as hers. "Why don't we sit outside awhile?"

Why hadn't he taken the embrace any further? Heck of a time for him to develop scruples on the subject, she thought.

Carrying their glasses, the bottle of wine and Eloise's apple, they descended to the patio exit. "This should be safe enough," Claude said as he pulled up a deck chair for her, "even if someone's watching the house." They sat in the dark under overhanging eaves, where any observer would have to get exactly the right angle to see them at all. Because the pre-dawn fog was still hours away, they had a glorious view of the star-sprinkled sky and the ocean bisected by a ribbon of moonlight. A cool breeze ruffled her hair.

"Who could be watching? Didn't you say nobody knows about this house?" She munched on apple slices while he filled the goblets. His fingers brushed hers when he handed her the glass. Flinching away from the contact, she splashed wine over the rim. Blushing, she wiped her hand on her jeans. The flush of warmth on her face and neck crept down her chest all the way to her stomach and thighs.

"I said it hasn't been publicized. It's hardly top secret. The stalker, if you want to call him that, could find the place if he tried hard enough. I'm hoping he won't manage to."

"I still think you're overreacting. After all, you're the one he's out to get, not me. If anything, he seemed to be warning me, not threatening." She took a bite of apple and a sip of wine, a light, semisweet Riesling that harmonized well with the taste of the fruit. "How long do you expect me to stay here anyway?"

"I wouldn't mind having you stay indefinitely." He lifted her hand, planted a light tongue-flick of a kiss on it then quickly released it.

When she glanced up, startled, she thought she saw a glint of red reflected in his eyes. Since he instantly looked away, she couldn't double-check. It had to be an optical illusion. *Oh, boy, maybe that cabernet was stronger than I thought.* "As much as I'd enjoy a life of luxury as a prisoner in your castle by the sea," she said with an attempt at a light touch, "I do have my own life and work to get back to." Doubtless that word "indefinitely" meant nothing anyway. The man was an actor, expert at charming people with empty phrases.

"So you do. Our script, for one thing."

"You seem pretty sure it'll get filmed," she ventured, hoping she didn't sound pushy for trying to pin him down.

"It will. The backers I mentioned owe me a favor."

"Do you plan to direct as well as produce and star?"

He laughed. "Deliver me from that! No, I have a director in mind, one who'll stick to my intentions for the tone of the thing."

"Such as not making Varney one of those spineless undead whining about his cursed existence," she teased, recalling what Claude had said on their first meeting.

"We'll have to tread a fine line, giving him a plausible motivation for suicide without turning him into just that."

"Well, I think it has to inspire him to a change of heart when he takes the risk of fleeing to the Bannerworths and Flora hides him from the mob," she said.

"Redeemed by the love of a good woman?" he said with a wry smile. He rested his fingers lightly on her wrist, as if counting her pulse. It sped up accordingly.

"Not love." The word made Eloise's head buzz like a nest of hornets. He didn't mean a thing by it. He was only making conversation about a pulp horror novel. "She thinks of him more as a friend, since he stopped pressuring them to sell the house and showed her where to find the secret cache of jewels to pay off the family's debt."

"Oh, yes, I almost forgot about the hidden treasure."

"After she helps him escape through the secret passage—"

"There's a secret passage too?" Laughter tinged the question.

"Sure, you can't have a Gothic mansion and a hidden treasure without a secret passage," said Eloise. "Then he sneaks to the home of the local vicar and confesses his evil past. The vicar assures Varney he's not beyond forgiveness, and he decides the only way to redeem himself is by seeking the true death."

"Romantic fiction aside, do you believe a vampire can be redeemed?" said Claude in an oddly serious tone.

"Theoretically, if they existed?" She shrugged. "If they had consciousness, instead of being demon-animated corpses, they would have free will too. So they could choose goodness. And if God made everything, He must have made vampires for a reason, if only to remind us ordinary human beings that we're not the rulers of the universe. So I'd think He would accept a vampire who repented."

"Well, when you put it that way, it's only fair. The trouble with the usual scenario is that your average vampire in search of redemption wants to be 'cured.' If a supernatural predator decides to mend his ways and stop ripping the occasional victim to shreds, why should the package have to include renouncing all those 'creature of the night' fringe benefits?"

"Like immortality and assorted super-powers? Good point."

"And invading the bedchambers of nubile maidens." With a fingernail, he traced a circle on the back of her hand. It seared like a lambent flame.

"Definitely an important perk." She tried to maintain a light tone, though she had trouble catching her breath.

"Next time, let's write a script about a vampire or some other dark-prowling predator who doesn't have to get cremated in a volcano," Claude said. "Here's to creatures of the night."

She raised her glass to clink with his. "I'll drink to that." Her nerves fizzed with delight at the hint of a "next time."

They finished the bottle in silence except for stray remarks now and then. When she stood up, Eloise felt a pleasant floating sensation but no actual drowsiness, after sleeping more than half the day. As a writer, she liked to keep a late schedule whenever she could anyway. Nighttime held fewer distractions, such as the afternoon and early evening plague of telemarketers, not to mention friends who mistook "working at home" for doing nothing.

"Would you care to watch a movie?" Claude said as they went inside, his hand under her elbow to guide her. "Unless you're too tired? Maybe you'd rather go to bed."

She felt a quiver in the pit of her stomach. Go to bed and dream of his hands, his mouth, his body covering hers? She eased her arm out of his gentle clasp, hoping he didn't notice how shaky her balance still was. "No, not at all. Do you have tapes of your own films?"

"Living near Los Angeles, you must know actors' egos better than that. Of course I do. Maybe you'd like to see the director's cut of the first Count Orloff opus?"

She agreed. They spent most of what remained of the night watching that video and its sequel. To her vague disappointment, Claude stayed on his side of the couch throughout both movies. True, she wasn't eager to face the decision of whether to maintain a dignified shield or melt into his arms. On the other hand, she didn't relish the implication that he'd lost interest in her body. Did his occasional sharp glance at her during the delectably romantic moments in the films mean he guessed how the scenes affected her? Could he somehow sense the flutter in her stomach, the pulsation between her legs, the trickle of wetness when he seemed about to move toward her and the letdown she felt when he returned his attention to the TV?

At the door of her room, she thought for a second that he wanted to revive the spark between them. His hands alighted on her upper arms, moving up and down the bare flesh in a distracted manner he seemed hardly aware of. He bent over her, his mouth hovering near hers. She parted her lips and waited. Emitting a long sigh, he kissed her cheek and drew back. A knot of frustration coiled low in her abdomen.

"Why don't you work up a few more pages of dialogue?" he said in a husky voice better suited to sensuality than business. "I'll be interested to see how you visualize those conversations between Varney and Flora."

"Okay," she murmured, involuntarily swaying toward him. "If you'll read the lines with me to check how it sounds."

"With pleasure." He let go of her so abruptly that she almost stumbled. "Sleep well, *chérie*." His voice caressed her. He spoiled the impression though by adding, "And remember, after you get up, stay inside the house."

"Will you cool it with the ominous prohibitions? You make me feel like Bluebeard's bride!" She retreated into the bedroom, closing the door with a firm click that didn't quite rate as a slam.

Chapter Eight

he next day, she again woke before Claude. She remembered a note in his publicity bio that his career had started in legitimate theater. That experience must have given him a permanent fondness for keeping late hours. After breakfast, she tackled the pivotal character-changing scenes she and Claude had discussed. Hours flew by while she typed page after page of dialogue. She had no trouble putting seductive speeches in Varney's mouth when she visualized him as Claude.

Dream on, girl, she cautioned herself. *Any day now you'll have to go home and turn back into a pumpkin.* She couldn't fool herself that Claude's flattery and seduction meant anything to him beyond a temporary diversion. Judging from the way he'd behaved the night before, he must have already regretted their intimacies at the con. No doubt her unconscious mind approved, because she'd had no erotic dreams this time. Her nipples puckered at the memory of that vivid dream the previous night. She crossed her arms over her breasts to stifle the feeling.

By five o'clock, though, she fidgeted with restlessness that made hash of her concentration. Given Claude's obvious resolution to keep distance between them, what gave him the right to forbid her to leave the house? She would take a walk on the beach if she darn well pleased. Especially since the day was almost over, and he still showed no signs of emerging from his cave.

Snatching an apple from the kitchen, she stomped out the patio door and down the steps to the beach. She scuffed through the sand to the seaweed-strewn rocks at the edge of the water and crunched her way through the fruit. By the time she buried the core, the exercise and sea air had cooled her temper a little. So what if Claude saw her as a writer instead of a sex object? Wasn't that what she'd originally preferred? And if he had a controlling streak, she could live with that for another day or two. If he delivered orders, she didn't have to obey them. The important thing was that the check, figuratively speaking, was in the mail.

Just as she considered going inside, a white shape caught her eye. A man walking across the beach toward her. He must have descended the steps while she'd been looking the other way. When he got closer, she saw that he wore a white suit, a straw hat and, of all things, white gloves. Tall—well, at five feet four, she thought of most men as tall—with untidy dark hair, he looked scarecrow-thin even in a jacket with padded shoulders.

He strolled right up to her and tipped his hat like a gentleman in an old movie. Now she could see that he had a neatly trimmed mustache, which, along with the suit and hat, gave him a barbershop-quartet appearance, somewhat spoiled by the sunglasses he also wore. "Miss Kern?" he said.

"Do I know you?"

"No, but I've been looking for you. I'm deeply concerned that you're staying in Claude Darvell's house." His suave tone held no hint of a threat.

Nevertheless, her heart accelerated. She folded her arms and took a step backward. "You're the one who called me the other night. What do you want?"

He spread his hands. "Only to help you. You are in danger as long as you're within his reach."

"Sorry, I don't find vague threats very convincing." Could she evade him and run for the house? He stood between her and the stairs. If she tried to dash around him, he could probably catch her in seconds with those long legs.

"Miss Kern, are you a Christian?"

She gaped at him. Was he a religious fanatic as well as a crazed stalker? "Well, yes, I belong to a church." Next, she expected, he would ask if she were saved. That always struck her as an intrusively personal question, along the lines of "Do you love your husband?"

Instead, he asked, "Do you have a crucifix with you?"

"Uh, no, left mine at home." *Okay, that settles it, certified nut.*

"Then you must accept this." From his coat pocket he produced a silver crucifix on a chain.

She stared at the minutely detailed Christ figure. "For goodness' sake, why?"

"Trust me, Miss Kern. I have known Claude for many years. He is a demon in human form. You need this for protection."

"You're out of your mind." She dodged around him and

sprinted for the steps. Or tried to, with the sand dragging at her feet.

He darted into her path and grabbed her arm. "Please, I don't intend to hurt you. Listen to me!"

"I don't have to listen to any of this insanity!" She tried to pull free, but her efforts hadn't the slightest effect on his grip.

"Claude killed my beloved."

Astonished, she forgot to struggle. "He what?"

"He caused her death. He's dangerous to women."

"How did he cause it? Not that I believe a word of this."

"He is a vampire. A bloodthirsty demon who only appears human. He lurks in the shadows and sucks the life out of inno-cent women."

Though her heart still hammered with fear, disgust kept her from outright panic. "Couldn't you come up with a more original fantasy? You've seen too many movies."

His brow furrowed in apparent confusion. "This has noth-ing to do with movies. I'm telling you the truth for your pro-tection." With the hand that still had the silver chain looped around it, he took off the sunglasses. His eyes pierced hers. "Listen carefully and do as I say."

A wave of faintness swept over Eloise, as if the sun's glare had caught up with her. Her fear evaporated.

The man's voice sounded like an echo reverberating through a tunnel. "Take the cross. Test it for yourself. Go into Claude's lair while he sleeps and place the holy symbol on his flesh. You will see that I'm right."

That didn't seem like too much to ask. In fact, the sug-gestion sounded quite reasonable. "Okay," she muttered. "But you can't be right. No such thing as vampires."

"Make the test and form your own conclusion. Then, for your safety, get away from here as soon as you can."

"Sure, whatever you say."

She felt him press the crucifix into her hand. A minute later, she found herself alone, climbing the steps to the house. The man had vanished.

Feeling as if her head were floating, she drifted upstairs to Claude's closed bedroom door. With the cross dangling from her fingers, she opened the door and tiptoed inside. Still in a daze, she walked through a sitting room into the bedroom beyond. She came to a halt beside Claude's bed, dimly visible in the heavily curtained chamber. He lay on his back, so still she couldn't see him breathing.

Her brain snapped into focus. She blinked, waiting for her eyes to adjust to the low light. *What the heck am I doing, barging into his bedroom?* Still, without conscious decision, she turned back the covers and extended the cross toward his bare chest.

The symbol grazed his skin. His eyes snapped open, blazing crimson. The air around him rippled. His face blurred into a dark-furred, tigerish mask, with fangs and pointed ears. With a wordless snarl, he clamped onto her wrists.

She let out a shriek and tried to pull away. His claws held her like a pair of handcuffs.

The next instant, he morphed back to normal. No fangs, no claws, no fur. In his eyes, though, pinpoints of red still gleamed.

Swallowing her heart, Eloise blinked, trying to convince herself that his eyes didn't shine. They did.

"Bloody hell!" He released one of her hands, the one holding the silver chain. "Get that thing away from me!"

She dropped the cross on the nightstand. Since he still held her tightly by one arm, she couldn't run away. Even if he'd let go, she thought she probably wouldn't be able to move. The few seconds of transformation had stunned her like a punch in the head.

Before she could catch her breath, Claude flipped her onto her back and pinned her with his body. "What in hell possessed you to do that?"

Her rib cage seemed to compress her lungs like a corset of steel. She had to gulp air to squeeze out an answer. "A man on the beach. Gave me the cross, told me to test you. Seemed like a good idea at the time."

"On the—? Damn it, I ordered you to stay inside!"

His anger swept over her like a gale-force wind. She summoned her own outrage to beat it back. "I don't take orders!"

He twined his fingers in her hair. When she struggled to escape his burning stare, he tightened his grip to keep her head immobile. Conscious of his weight on her, she felt her stomach churn with a mix of fear and excitement.

"Oh, damn, your heart's pounding. You're afraid of me."

"Well, yeah, I'm not stupid." A half-hysterical giggle escaped her.

He loosened his grip and smoothed her hair. "I have no intention of ripping your throat out."

"That's a relief. What are you going to do?" Now that the immediate terror had faded, she became aware of his legs trapping hers, her breasts against his chest and his face inches from her own.

"I should make you forget all this."

"Vampire mind control? Haven't you done enough of that already? You hypnotized me at the con, didn't you?" His silence confessed to the charge. "If I wanted a man to manipulate me and order me around, I'd have stuck to that guy I broke up with in grad school." She dug her nails into his shoulders.

He winced. "I was only trying to protect you. Philip—the stalker—could have killed you."

"He didn't do one thing to threaten me. He just talked crazy. Anyway, why would you care if I get hurt?"

"Damn it, woman, of course I care!" He tangled his fingers in her hair again. When she gasped, he covered her open mouth with his. His tongue thrust inside, grazing her teeth.

The swirl of his tongue around the inside of her lips sent sparks dancing along her nerves. She squirmed under him, eager to feel the pressure of his body on her tender parts.

He broke off the kiss, heaving ragged breaths. "I promised myself I would not do that." He sat up, with the sheet still covering him from the hips down. As far as she could see, he didn't wear anything in bed. "We need to talk."

"We certainly do." She sat up too, her head reeling and her cheeks hot with the brew of emotions that simmered in her. "Truth?"

"Very well, *ma chérie*. The whole truth and nothing but. Not here though. Go into the next room and let me get dressed first." He cupped her chin to raise her eyes to his. "You won't run away, I trust?"

Run where? "Not a chance."

Eloise retreated into the adjacent sitting room. After opening the curtains halfway to let in some light, she saw a matching couch and chair, a bookcase, a miniature refrigerator and a wet bar with a compact-model microwave oven on its counter. She sat on the couch and waited, glad for the few minutes of solitude to tame the hive of bees in her skull and the spiders skittering in her stomach.

Soon Claude emerged from the bedroom, barefoot, in a pair of blue satin jogging shorts and a T-shirt. He went to the bar, filled a glass with ice and got out bottles of gin and tonic. "Care for a drink?"

"No, thanks, I want my head clear. If that's possible around you." She glared at him.

"Well, I need one." When she flinched, he added with a wry smile, "Not that kind. Not right this minute anyway." After he'd mixed his gin and tonic, he took a seat at the other end of the couch from her, out of the direct sunlight from the window. "Tell me exactly what happened when you met Philip."

She summarized the encounter. "He said you're a vampire, a demon in human shape, as he put it. I'm not sure how it happened, but the next thing I knew, I was in here testing the theory."

"Of course," Claude sighed. "I should have known. He caught you off guard, so he hypnotized you. I should have known you wouldn't do anything like that on a mere suggestion. Regardless of what you saw just now, I'm not a demon."

"You changed—" Her breath caught in her throat, cutting off the words.

"I apologize for that. A defense mechanism. You startled me out of a sound sleep, after all."

"What about the cross?"

"A psychosomatic reaction. I'm not a creature of the devil, and I'm not undead either. Though if you'd looked for a pulse a few minutes ago, you'd have had trouble finding one. Suspended animation looks a lot like death."

She folded her arms in resistance to his reasonable tone. "I don't hear you denying you're a vampire."

"I don't deny it." He took a swallow of his drink. "But I'm not supernatural. We're another species, long-lived, with a specialized diet."

"Liquid protein."

He nodded.

Her numbed brain woke up and processed clues from the past few days. "Oh, God, you drank my blood! How many times?"

He gazed into his glass as if embarrassed.

"Come on, level with me. At the con?"

"Yes, and the night before last, after we arrived here."

A flush spread over her body. "Then all those feelings I thought were dreams came from you? And that's why I can't remember much about Saturday night?"

"Granted." He drained his glass and got up to mix another drink, heavy on the gin.

Her throat tightened with indignation. "You—I don't believe this! You made up all that rigmarole about producing my script just to feed on me."

"What?" He whirled around to face her, glass in hand. "Bloody hell, do you seriously think I'd go to all that trouble just for a little refreshment? I can get that from the vampire groupies."

Her pulse hammered in her temples. "Well, isn't that what I am to you?"

"Eloise, no!" He hurried to the couch and sat near her. She edged as far away as the space allowed. "I feasted on your mind, your passions, not only your blood. That's why I didn't want to take any risk of letting Philip see us together. He would realize instantly that I care for you. And I meant it when I said I'd like to have you stay here."

"How can I tell what you mean? You turned me into a puppet, like one of those blow-up sex dolls, and wiped my memory on top of it. Anyway, you're an actor. You could turn on the charm at will even if you weren't a vampire."

"Please, *ma belle*, let me prove that isn't true." He caressed her shoulder and gazed into her eyes. In this light, his no longer glowed red, but they still held an inhuman sheen of silver that she could hardly believe she'd missed before.

She jerked away from his touch. "Don't look at me."

"I've vowed not to mesmerize you again."

"I don't trust your vows. Not yet."

He stalked to the bar and leaned against it, half-turned away from her. "Very well, I'm not looking at you. Now will you listen?"

"I'm listening. What do you mean, you vowed not to do it again?"

"I want you as a friend, an equal." He gave a dry chuckle. "Something we don't say to ephemerals very often. Many of my people would think I'm going soft even to consider it."

"Ephemerals? That's what you call us? Here today, gone tomorrow. No wonder you think you can treat us like puppets."

"I don't." He gritted his teeth with a muted growl. "Some ephemerals. Not you."

"Well, at least you admit it." A new thought chilled her. "How many people have you killed?"

"Oh, for hell's sake!" He slammed the glass on the bar. "I don't kill for food. I take no more than they can spare, and I reward them with pleasure. Pleasure that I thoroughly enjoy sharing. I've killed in self-defense now and then. Not often. I told you, I prefer the quiet life."

"That Philip guy said you killed his beloved, or caused her death anyway. Is that how he knows you're a vampire?"

"What do you think *he* is?"

"He's one too?" Speechless for a minute, Eloise sorted out this new bit of data. "Wait a second, he walked around in broad daylight."

"You've read enough books like *Dracula* and *Varney*, not to mention reams of folklore, that you shouldn't believe that tripe about vampires bursting into flame in the sun."

"Yeah, but he was out on the beach with no shade at all."

"Goes to show how much he's willing to suffer for the satisfaction of harassing me," said Claude. "How was he dressed?"

"White suit, gloves, hat, sunglasses."

"You see? Probably sunscreen as well. I could walk on the beach in that costume too but I wouldn't enjoy it much."

"What about the cross? It didn't seem to bother him."

Claude fidgeted with his glass as if self-conscious about the topic. "I suffer from a phobia for religious objects. He doesn't. He was fortunate enough to grow up in the enlightened atmosphere of Victorian England. I was born in a French village in 1738, when rural folk still seriously believed demons might walk among them. It was also the height of the vampire-hunting craze in Greece and Eastern Europe, as you know. I became infected with the superstitions of the culture around me."

"Really? Does that happen a lot?"

"It can. We're highly adaptable, especially in childhood. We have to be to fit invisibly into your world. We tend to pick up human attitudes unless our mentors are very careful." He sat down, more relaxed now but still making a point of not looking directly at her. "It still happens to some young vampires today if they're allowed to watch horror movies."

She had to laugh at the image of stern vampire elders censoring their children's viewing habits. "Tell me about Philip. Who was the woman, and why does he blame you for her death?"

Claude sighed. "He's not far wrong, but I never intended her any harm. I suppose I'd better tell you the whole story."

"Yes, please do." She folded her arms and frowned at him, determined to shield herself against his charm until he offered her some basis for trust.

Chapter Nine

s I said, I grew up in France. I stayed there until the Revolution, when I relocated to England. I had no desire to meet Madame Guillotine. Decapitation kills us as easily as you. In the middle of the nineteenth century, I wandered into an acting career mostly out of boredom. I discovered that I enjoyed performing before audiences. Their emotions could be quite—intoxicating." He smiled like a cat licking milk from its whiskers. "If you researched the late Victorian theatrical world in depth, you might stumble across an obscure actor named Claude D'Arnot."

"You."

He nodded. "If you noticed the photographs and posters in my office, you must have guessed by now that all those ancestors of mine were actually myself."

"And you hang the pictures in plain sight? In a vampire movie, that would be my first clue that you're immortal."

He laughed. "In real life, of course, nobody nowadays would come up with that theory. They'd think what you probably did: 'What an amazing family resemblance.' Right?"

"Well, yeah."

"That's part of my camouflage. Who could suspect I would display my past lives that brazenly if I really were immortal? But all that came after the story I'm telling you now," he continued. "By the 1890s I'd temporarily given up the stage. I became involved with a young woman who practiced as a medium. I helped her get out from under the thumb of her charlatan of an uncle who used her in spiritualist scams. She knew my true nature, and we stayed together for several years."

"Were you in love with her?" Eloise tried to convince herself that she asked from mere curiosity, not because she cared about Claude's past liaisons.

"That's a human emotion. I'm not sure I know what it means. I was addicted to her, the inevitable result of feeding from the same donor for any length of time. In an exclusive relationship like that, the roots strike very deep."

"Exclusive? How could she stand the blood loss?"

He sighed. "We don't come close to draining our donors. I don't need more than a few sips when the emotions are so intense. Quality makes up for quantity. Bulk nourishment comes from animals."

"Okay, you had an addictive relationship." Eloise felt sick at the implication that he might think of her too as some sort of drug. "Where does Philip come in? Was that the woman he accused you of killing?"

"No, that was later. My donor began to have doubts about me. Intellectually, she knew I wasn't supernatural or demonic.

Emotionally, she couldn't quell the fear that her soul was somehow tainted. She wanted to break it off. Knowing neither of us could resist the lure of our mutual addiction, I had to get as far away from her as possible. I'd known Philip Trent in London for a few years, before he'd moved to San Francisco. He suggested I might enjoy living there, so I made the move in 1902."

"You were friends then."

"Yes, what I originally told you about him was essentially true, although not the whole truth. I decided it was time to assume a new identity, so I changed my name. I picked 'Darvell' because that was what my mother called herself at the time."

"You've got a mother?" she blurted out.

"Did you think we reproduced by spontaneous generation? She's dead though. The only family I have now is a half-brother. But you don't want to get sidetracked onto the subject of genealogy, do you?"

"Oh no." She made a mental note to satisfy her curiosity about vampire family structures some other time. "Go on about Philip."

"There I was in California, making a fresh start. I was determined never to get attached to another ephemeral. Not that my emotions had been engaged to any depth, or so I told myself, but the break was still painful. I plunged into the San Francisco night life with Philip, flitting from one lovely female blossom to another like a pair of honey-sipping wasps."

"I can imagine, rolling in money on top of that charm of yours," she said in a caustic tone to fend off the memory of how she'd felt when Claude had stung and sipped her.

"A few years after I joined him, Philip became enamored

of a woman, a naive ingénue he had no business fixating on. To cut short the distressing details, I didn't realize how he felt about the girl. We have a taboo against preying on someone else's donor. But I assumed he thought of her as a casual victim, so I ignored the rule."

"You claimed you'd never killed for food."

"Don't jump to conclusions. I didn't drain the girl." Claude got up and paced while he continued. "I got careless about erasing her memory. The next time Philip visited her, his bite triggered the recollection of mine."

"So then she figured out he was a vampire too?"

"Exactly. Of course, up to that point she'd been a rational young woman of the new century who would have laughed at the idea of vampires. She was terrified, thought she was losing her mind."

"I know the feeling," said Eloise, thinking of the moment when Claude's face had transformed into a raging beast's.

"That night, Philip stormed into my flat, furious about the way he'd had to leave her in hysterics. I handled the blasted thing all wrong. Instead of apologizing for my trespass, as vampire etiquette demanded, I made light of it. Asked him why he made such a fuss over an ephemeral. After all, he could always find another pet."

"Pet?" She almost choked on her indignation at the word.

"That's how most of our kind view their repeat donors. I had to pretend I thought that way, to keep from admitting to myself how the loss of my own 'pet' had hurt me."

"So how did Philip react?" She reserved judgment about his claim to have been hurt.

"Said he was in love with the young female. Of course, I laughed at the very idea. When he reacted by trying to throttle me, I had to take his infatuation seriously. I offered to talk to his young lady and undo the damage I'd done. Needless to say, he wasn't about to let me near her alone. We went to her place together."

He poured himself a straight shot of gin and gulped it down then resumed pacing. "I don't want to dwell on the details. We had to force our way in. When I tried to mesmerize her, she screamed and waved a cross in my face. Philip tried, and when he put his arms around her, she slapped him. He wouldn't use physical force on her, so when she ran outside, all we could do was chase her down the street."

"Why didn't the hypnotism work?"

Claude shrugged. "She had faith in the cross. It gave her a focus for resistance." He picked up a corkscrew from the bar and tossed it from one hand to the other. "She fled a couple of streets over, into a Catholic church. Philip followed her all the way to the altar. I stopped at the door. That was when the earthquake started."

"Oh! The big 1906 quake?"

He nodded, still fiddling with the corkscrew. "I shouted at Philip to run for it. He wouldn't leave the girl, and she ducked behind the altar and refused to go with him. When the roof collapsed, I cleared out."

"You mean they—"

"Both of them, buried in the rubble." He stabbed the corkscrew into the top of the bar, where it protruded like an arrow in a target. "After the quake, I went back to check. The whole church had crumbled into a heap of bricks."

Eloise's stomach knotted. She swallowed a mouthful of acid. "But Philip's alive."

"About a month ago, the church started a building program, which included archaeological excavation of the present parking lot. They found two bodies or, rather, a woman's skeleton and the strangely preserved body of a man."

"So he woke up? What would it take to kill a vampire permanently?"

"Decapitation, cremation, stake through the heart if it's left in place long enough. The usual." His lips quirked in a humorless smile. "Anything on the standard list except sunlight, which just gives us headaches that won't quit. Luckily for Philip, the falling debris didn't separate his head from his body or crush the brain beyond regeneration."

"And now he's out to get you."

"I'm afraid so." With a sigh he sat down with arms flung wide along the back of the couch. "To me, a long human lifetime has passed since the quake. To him, it's little more than yesterday. No wonder he's still furious."

"But you didn't kill his girlfriend, donor, whatever. If you helped to cause her death, so did he. You couldn't have predicted how she'd react, much less that an earthquake would hit right that minute." Eloise wasn't sure why she felt like defending Claude after the way he had treated her at the convention. "Anyway, it's a relief to find out you're not a murderer, much less a demon. I won't have to sell my soul to get my script produced."

He laughed. "And I'm relieved you haven't run out of here screaming in terror."

"It was close there for a while," she said. She still couldn't wrap her mind around the change she'd witnessed when the cross had grazed him.

"Unfortunately, it's clear Philip doesn't see the situation your way. I'm afraid he'll use you to punish me. He thinks

I destroyed the woman he loved, so what better way to get revenge than through someone I care about? The last thing I want is to see another ephemeral killed on my account, especially you."

"How could you possibly feel anything special about me? You hardly know me." She heard an edge of harshness in her own voice. It jolted her to realize how much she wished Claude did care about her.

"But I do know you. Intimately. For vampires, a night or two is all it takes. We can read emotions, remember?"

Shocked, she stared at him, met his intent gaze and hastily looked away. Her cheeks flushed. "You mean all that stuff about Varney sensing Flora's reaction wasn't just theoretical? You know every thought in my head?"

"Not thoughts," he said. "Emotions, sensations. For true telepathy, we would have to bond—share blood both ways."

She hid her face in her hands. "I don't believe this," she muttered. No wonder his lovemaking fulfilled her needs so perfectly. He saw, scented and tasted every impulse that flitted through her body and mind. "Oh, God, it's like you stripped me naked." Remembering how she'd awakened in her bed at the hotel, she said, "You did, but this is worse."

She hurried to the window, staring at the sun low on the horizon above the ocean. "How could you do that to me and then call me a friend? You—actor!"

"*Chérie*, please don't!" He crept up beside her and reached for her arm.

Shaking off the tentative touch, she said, "And don't try to charm me with bilingual sweet talk."

"Why does it upset you this badly? You enjoyed the encounters as much as I did."

"That's not the point." She swiped at the tears spilling from her eyes. "You played me like a musical instrument. You never gave me a chance to accept or refuse."

"Suppose I'd told you the truth from the beginning? Assuming you believed me, would you have leaped into my arms?"

"I don't know. And since you didn't take the risk of being honest, we'll never know."

"Didn't you understand when I said I'd vowed not to mesmerize you again? After I realized I wanted you as a companion, not just a food source or even a business associate, I stopped 'playing' you."

She could almost hear his teeth grind. "Confound it, Eloise, look at me!"

She turned in a slow circle toward him. Her breath rapid and shallow, she avoided his eyes. "You think it's that easy to make me trust you?"

"What can I do then?" Some emotion roughened his voice. She didn't dare let herself assume it was pain at her rejection.

"What did you change into when I touched you with the cross? Show me."

"Oh, hell, do you have to ask for that?" When she just glared at him, he said, "I apologize for the lapse in control. We have a limited ability to shape-change. It's an ancestral form encoded in the genes, a vestigial skill, not much use in the modern environment."

"Limited? No bats, wolves, clouds of mist?"

"Don't we wish," he chuckled. "No, just what you saw. Well, and a spot of levitation."

"That's all? Gosh, what a letdown." She maintained the sarcastic tone to shield herself from the attraction that could easily override her judgment. "Come on, demonstrate."

"Yes, that's all. Any elaborate transformations you might see are purely illusion, including a veil of invisibility that's almost as good as mist." He narrowed his eyes in concentration and faded from her sight. Before she could blink, he reappeared as a blurred outline then sharpened into solidity.

"Oh, wow." Gray patches gathered before her eyes. She stumbled backward to lean against the wall.

Folding his arms, he focused on a point somewhere past her shoulder and blurred again. A dark velvet pelt spread over his face and arms. His ears grew points, his eyes glowed red and fangs sprouted in his mouth. A shadow of silver wings momentarily hovered behind him. After a few seconds, the change reversed itself like a tape on rewind, and he reverted to normal. Stretching his arms wide, he rose from the floor and floated toward the ceiling. He drifted to the floor, where he stood with his hands extended toward her, palms up. "Please don't be afraid."

"I'm working on it." She reached out to run her fingertips over his right palm. "You're real. Not dreaming. Not crazy."

"No. I'm real." He shivered when she repeated the light touch. "Easy."

"Hey, little hairs." The folktales had preserved the facts about vampires in random hit-or-miss fashion, it seemed.

"Yes, and they're sensitive." He drew back and folded his arms. "If I can't touch or look at you, it's unfair for you to take advantage."

She couldn't decide whether he was teasing or serious. "How sensitive can they be, if you use your hands normally all the time?"

"Firm grasping doesn't trigger the response. Other kinds of touching do."

"Great, I have a way to get back at you for some of the things you did to me Saturday night." She clamped a lid on the turbulent images of those things.

He drew a hissing breath. "Does that mean you may allow it to happen again?"

"Don't push it!" she snapped.

"Very well." He backed up, hands raised in surrender. "I swore I'd leave your free will intact, and I won't break my word."

"Darn it, Claude, don't you have any idea how I feel, knowing you practically turned me inside out and hardly let me remember any of it?" After a pause for thought, she said, "Oh, yeah, you know everything I feel."

"I know you're angry and frustrated, understandably."

"Talk about unfair advantage!" She flung herself onto the couch. "Let me get this straight. You drank my blood, and that's like sex for you."

He sat down too, still keeping his distance. "We breed so infrequently that reproductive sex means very little to us. I've never been chosen as a stud, but I can't miss what I've never experienced. And it doesn't matter that a male vampire can't mate with a human female. We get our satisfaction from our donors' arousal and fulfillment."

"The emotion-reading thing." She couldn't suppress a mental flashback to her "dream" of the other night. A shadow of that excitement tingled through her body.

"I told you I feasted on your passion. Those of our kind who have produced offspring say the blood-sharing is far more intense than ordinary sex."

"And you made me forget the whole thing." She gulped a deep breath to gather her nerve. "If you want to make up for lying and manipulating, you can start by doing it all over, with me fully conscious."

He became very still. "Eloise, are you sure you want this?"

"Why not? You said you don't take enough to do any harm." She hugged herself, feeling as if her heart might burst out of her rib cage.

"It's harm to our relationship that concerns me. Don't tempt me into this if you might regret it."

She shook her head. "Why worry about closing the barn door after the horse goes to water?"

"The more often we indulge," he said, "the easier it will be for Philip to notice my mark on your aura. It'll be obvious that I have a special interest in you. I don't want to make you a target."

"If we're supposed to be friends and equals and all that, I get some input on that decision too."

"Damn. I never did develop the habit of resisting temptation." He ran his fingers through his hair, got up and paced to the bar and back. "What you should do is leave right now. Call a cab, go to the airport in Monterey and catch the first flight south. Make Philip think you took his advice and rejected me. Then he'll leave you alone."

"What if I don't want to leave right now?" She stood up, hands on her hips.

Claude took a step toward her, reached for her, let his arms drop and then, with an inarticulate growl, grabbed her. "We'll discuss it later."

He pulled her to him and captured her mouth with a hard kiss. She gasped in a spasm of alarm. She knew he must hear and feel the hammering of her heart.

He raised his head to impale her with his violet-silver, red-tinged eyes. "You are afraid. I won't continue if you have doubts."

Wrapping her arms around his waist, Eloise shook her head. "Not afraid, just startled. I don't have doubts. I want to experience this. But slower."

He rubbed up and down her spine as if petting a kitten. "Yes. Forgive me for pouncing so hard." Easing her head onto his chest, he stroked her hair and sighed. "It's been so long since I've enjoyed a woman who's fully aware. I got carried away. You know, you'll still have to leave sometime within the next day or so. We have to get Philip off your trail."

Was he trying to get rid of her? She looked up at him. While he could read her emotions, she had no clue as to his. "Okay, whatever, just call me Scarlett." When he quizzically raised his eyebrows, she said, "I'll think about it tomorrow."

"Very well, I can't refuse a lady's wishes. Where? Couch or bed?"

Her breath caught in her throat. "Bed. Yours. You invaded mine enough already."

Chapter Ten

e picked her up and carried her into the other room. She kicked off her sandals on the way. Placing her on the satin sheets, he removed the tie from her ponytail and ran his fingers through her hair, making her scalp tingle. When he rolled up the hem of her T-shirt, she said, "Wait. You have to undress too."

"Why? I told you ordinary intercourse doesn't happen." His fingers skimmed the waistband of her shorts. His cool skin on hers made her shiver.

"Equality. If I have to be exposed, so do you."

"Fair enough. Come to think of it, skin-to-skin contact sounds very pleasant." He peeled off his shirt. "Your aura glows red with heat. I want to bathe in it."

His resonant voice made her insides vibrate, like feeling the notes of a pipe organ through the floorboards. "And I need to see better," she whispered. "Need light."

The heavy drapes made the room dim even now. When the sun finished setting, it would be too dark for her. Claude, she suspected, could see like a cat.

"No electric light," he said. "Too harsh." He opened the nightstand drawer and produced a fat candle, which he set in an ashtray and lit. The scent of vanilla wafted from it. "That should last several hours." He removed his shorts and sat on the edge of the bed.

Eloise scanned his lean, pale body in the candlelight. An inverted triangle of fine hair covered his chest from the nipples down, tapering to a point at the navel. From there, a thin line of hair arrowed down to the groin, where his cock lay at rest against his thigh. A shuddering breath escaped from her. Her abdominal muscles tensed, but not with fear, when his fingers crept under her T-shirt. He rolled it up, the backs of his hands brushing her skin, skimming the inside curves of her breasts.

She lifted her arms to let him pull the shirt over her head then leaned on her elbows to give him access to the hooks at the back of her bra. When he tossed it aside with the shirt, a draft from the air conditioner raised prickles on her skin. His fingertips brushed her neck, swept down between her breasts and settled at her waist, creating a fresh wave of shivers. Wetness pooled between her legs. Could he tell how aroused she was? Of course, he sensed everything she felt. A flush suffused her body.

He spread his hand on the bare skin just above her beltline. "When blood rushes to your skin that way, it's all I can do to wait." He rubbed her middle in a circular motion with the lightest possible contact. "Your warmth makes my palms tingle. If only you could see how your aura turns deep red here when you become excited." He moved down the front of her shorts to the apex of her thighs. "And you smell delicious."

She couldn't suppress a wiggle of her hips. "So taste me."

He bent over and licked first the right nipple then the left, each in one long stroke. The heat of his tongue contrasted with the near chill of his hands, one of which explored her inner thighs while the other cupped her mound.

"Not fair," she gasped. "I want to drive you crazy too."

"You already do." He unzipped her shorts, and she raised her hips to let him strip them off. Reclining beside her, he leaned on one elbow to tickle the inside of her legs just below the nest of curls.

She grabbed his hand and ran her thumb over the delicate hairs in the palm. "How does that feel?"

He closed his eyes. "Maddening. If you want me to go slowly, don't do that." He freed his hand and returned it to the space between her legs. One finger grazed her inner lips. She felt herself melting.

"Are you hypnotizing me now?"

He nuzzled her neck. "I promised not to."

"Then how do you do this?" He probed her slit, which throbbed eagerly. She squeezed her legs shut on his hand.

"I stir the currents of your aura. I follow the path of your arousal. I feel exactly when your excitement rises." He spread a sheen of wetness up to her clit. "I feel you want me to touch you here." His fingers swirled around the tight knot of sensation and zeroed in on the spot where it burned hottest. He echoed her earlier question. "How does that feel?"

"You know how," she said through gritted teeth. "You read my emotions."

"But only from the outside." He lapped each of her nipples again then abandoned the aching peaks to lick her throat. "We're not bonded, so I can't share your sensations from inside. What does human arousal feel like?"

"Like my skin's on fire. Especially there." Sparks danced from his flickering tongue at her neck to her taut nipples and the swollen bud where his fingers played. "Like I'm melting into a puddle of hot lava. And tight. Like my clit's about to burst."

His teeth stung her throat. A rush of warmth quenched the minor pain and transformed it to a bolt of electricity that zapped from that spot straight to the center of her need. He responded to the arching of her hips with a frenzied rubbing of her clit. His fingers plunged inside her. The suction of his lips at her neck pushed her over the edge. Her clit pulsed like a second heartbeat, and her sheath convulsed to the same rhythm.

Still lapping her blood, he lay on top of her, tucking one leg between hers. The pressure gave her all the stimulation she needed to shudder through wave after wave of overlapping climaxes that seemed to last forever.

Finally, when she felt ready to faint from sensory overload, he stopped drinking, with one last flicker of his tongue. He rolled on his side, bringing her with him in a tight hug.

After a few minutes, her head stopped spinning. "I see what you mean about addictive."

His breath ruffled her hair. "Yes, and I'm afraid I've already gone past the point of no return with you. After this, nobody else could satisfy me."

"Did it really feel as incredible to you as it did to me?"

"Oh, yes." She heard amusement in his voice. "Probably more."

"I can't imagine how. Especially if you don't even feel anything, well, down there."

"What gives you that idea? The sensation centers on tasting your blood, but it involves my whole body. Every inch of my skin becomes hypersensitive. When you spend, I ride the wave with you. If you could imagine what it's like to feel your heart pounding, feel your hot flesh pressed against mine . . . Damn, I'm getting thirsty again."

She giggled. "Nothing wrong with that. I'm still here." She reached between them to stroke his chest. The hair felt like velvet. She traced it to his navel and below. When he didn't object, she fondled his quiescent penis. "So you don't mind this?"

"I like it. I enjoy any contact with you. This is new to me though. Never had a donor touch me there before."

"Really? Why not?"

"There was no reason to." He ran his hand down her spine to explore the curve of her derriere. "Ah, like silk. I've never been naked with a donor before."

She tilted her head to look into his half-closed eyes. If true, that statement added weight to his claim that he thought of her as special. She squeezed his shaft. It began to harden. "I thought you said you can't—perform—with human females."

"Again, never had any reason to try. I don't produce or expel sperm. But, as you see, direct stimulation does have an effect."

She made a cylinder of her palm and pumped up and down his shaft. It became engorged. She heard a rumble in his chest that almost sounded like a purr. "If you wanted to, we could, well, you know." Suddenly shy, Eloise paused in her caresses. What if he found the idea unappealing? If so, she didn't want to coax him into the act.

"We could couple. Interesting." He thrust into her hand. "Please continue. That's giving me a hell of an appetite."

The husky note in his voice stirred a tingle between her legs, followed by a new gush of wetness. She pressed her thighs together to ease the tickle in her clit.

He nuzzled her neck and growled deep in his chest, making her nerves quiver. "You're ready again. The fragrance of your nectar makes me so thirsty I can't stand it." He licked the hollow of her throat then traced a path to the inside of her right breast. He nipped the skin. The now-familiar jolt of electricity convulsed her.

Squirming, she rubbed up and down his shaft. She draped her leg over his, desperate for contact to relieve the ache.

The frantic lapping of his tongue paused. "What do you want? Tell me."

Hell of a time to pretend he can't sense it! Between labored breaths, she said, "Rub me—there—before I explode!"

His fingers matched the rhythm of his tongue, and she did explode. "Come in! Please!" When he didn't obey instantly, she shoved him from his side to his back and rolled on top. Ignoring the smile that flitted across his lips, she knelt above him and pointed his cock at her hole. "Now!" She lowered herself on him, and he plunged in to the hilt.

Claude gasped in delighted astonishment at Eloise's sudden attack. The hot, silken wetness that surrounded his shaft made currents radiate from that point throughout his body in expanding waves of excitement. He wanted to plunge still deeper into her, swim in her life-force, merge with her until her energy flowed in all his veins and filled each empty spot to the brim.

She rocked, rubbing her clitoris against the hair at the root of his cock. Her sheath slid up and down on his rod in a smooth rhythm that made his teeth tingle with the need to taste her. He sensed her excitement swelling toward release. Her inner muscles rippled around him. She skimmed her nails over his chest. Tormented by the light contact, he growled, "Harder!" She scratched him, but still not hard enough. When he hissed aloud, she slashed, leaving fiery tracks that made his stomach cramp with need.

His mouth watered and his jaws ached. He couldn't let her spend without him. He needed to soar with her again.

With a roar, he gripped her arms. "Damn it, I can't reach you!"

She let him pull her into a tight embrace, their bodies pressed together from shoulders to loins. His mouth fastened on her throat. When her blood flowed over his tongue, it completed a circuit of energy that poured through both of them in an endless circle of arousal and satisfaction. Another climax ripped through her, and he shuddered along with her. She screamed, and he echoed her with a howl of ecstasy.

Mine! he exulted. *Mine, forever!* No one else could touch her. If he had to, he would kill to keep her safe.

He felt her go limp, pleasantly exhausted, on the edge of fainting. Her aura faded to a rose-tinged pastel. He shifted position to pillow her head on his shoulder until the fog cleared from her mind.

"Don't worry," he murmured. "You haven't lost much blood. The exhaustion you feel is the energy drain. And the incisions will heal in a day or two, much faster than ordinary cuts."

"I'm not worried." She rubbed her face against his chest. "That was incredible."

"*Vraiment*! I never imagined the insertion of one append-age into an orifice could enhance the experience that way." A ghost of the ardor they had just shared warmed his blood, and he heard her pulse quicken too.

She punched him lightly on the arm. "Ephemerals aren't so inferior after all."

"I never considered you inferior. Merely different."

She sat up. "You used to though, didn't you?"

"I don't deny that I've considered all my past donors as sources of refreshment or, at most, pets. But not you. Not from the first night we met." He fought against the impulse to use his hypnotic power to override her doubts. He wanted her fully aware, free and willing in their union.

"I don't like the idea that you think of other people as lower animals either." Bitterness tinged her voice.

"For you, I'll try to reform." When she frowned at his flip-pant tone, he said more seriously, "It's not easy to change the habits of a couple of centuries, but I do want to please you. For your sake, I'll revise my attitude toward the rest of your spe-cies." Already that "revision" had begun, he realized, for now he understood Philip's anger and grief over his lover's death.

She started collecting her clothes. "You talk as if we have a future. Aside from making a movie together, I mean."

Though he still sensed her reservations, he decided further argument right now would have only a negative effect. He sat up with the sheet across his lap. "I hope so, *chérie*. Dozens of movies and a very long future—after we deal with Philip. Look, you need nourishment. We'll discuss it downstairs over dinner."

The thought of letting her go, even temporarily, chilled him. He wanted to share thousands of nights like this. He wanted a lifetime to explore her vibrant mind, bask in her scintillating aura and feast on her intoxicating elixir. But first he had to ensure her safety.

After a shower, she joined him in the kitchen. He served her another of the frozen dinners and poured himself a glass of milk. She gaped at it. "Vampires drink milk?"

"Animal blood and milk form the bulk of our diet. Surely you've come across that detail in folklore?"

She recalled a few tales that accused vampires of drying up the milk of the village cows. "Sheesh, another blow to my romantic fantasies. Okay, what about Philip? Can't you do anything about him?"

"Such as? We're forbidden to kill our own kind except in self-defense. I talked to one of the elders after I found out about Philip's resurrection. I'm not getting cut any slack. Unless he attacks me directly, I can't destroy him without becoming an outcast."

"Oh."

"Not that I want to. He may be a blot on the landscape, but the poor chap was my friend once. The only way I can see to settle the problem without violence is, as I said, to convince him you're not important to me."

Am I? While she didn't want to whine for reassurance, she couldn't shake off the awareness that he had the whole emotion-reading advantage over her. "And if he doesn't give up harassing us?"

Claude shook his head. "If he wants to make a nuisance of himself, there's no practical way I can evade him. I'm astonished that he found me so fast to begin with. The elder I consulted was quick to point out that if I didn't live this 'purloined letter' lifestyle, Philip would probably never have known where to start looking."

Recognizing the title of the Poe mystery, Eloise said, "Purloined letter, hidden in plain sight. A vampire pretending to be an actor playing a vampire."

"Precisely. The strategy has the added bonus that if anyone notices my eccentricities, such as not eating and avoiding the sun, they're chalked up to publicity stunts."

"With the drawback that the few people who do know vampires exist have no trouble picking up the clues."

"Too true." He finished the milk and sat back in his chair. "I don't know what long-term solution we can arrange, but for now, he has to see you leave. He has to believe you consider me a monster. Then you should be safe."

"For how long?" She banged her fork on the table. "Do you expect me to stay away from you for a week? A month? Until another building falls on your ex-friend?"

"Eloise—" He reached for her hand. "I want you with me always. But not at the cost of your life."

She withdrew from his handclasp. "Am I supposed to leave right now?"

"In the middle of the night? Hardly. I'd feel safer if you wait until day, when he'll be weaker."

"What are we going to do for the rest of the night?" When the obvious answer popped into her mind, her cheeks warmed.

"Not what you're thinking." He stood up to clear the dishes. "Something to occupy our thoughts, so I can keep my hands—and other parts—off you."

Feeling a second or two of irrational letdown that he didn't plan to whisk her to the bedroom again, she said, "It can't stay this intense forever, can it? The attraction has to cool off eventually, and then what?"

"*Au contraire*, for all I've heard, the allure between vampire and donor doesn't fade like human infatuation. It only grows stronger with time. There's the addiction factor, you see. It's a biological phenomenon, not merely emotional."

"Addiction. Then how can we possibly know it's anything except biological?" The doubts she'd buried rose up once more. When he said he cared for her, he himself might not even know the truth of that claim.

"Considering how desperately I craved you after the first sip, long before the dependency could have started, I trust the reality of my feelings." Circling the table, he imprisoned her head between his hands and stared at her like a cat with a bird under its paw. "'Other women cloy the appetites they feed, but she makes hungry where most she satisfies.'"

"Shakespeare, now? I'm no Cleopatra."

"Believe that I see you that way, *ma belle*."

The pressure of his gaze made her pulse flutter in her throat. "You promised not to use hypnosis on me."

"I'm not. Perhaps you're already beginning to sense my emotions, even without a physical bond." His voice caressed her like a cool breeze on sun-warmed flesh.

"Well, put a lid on them. Let's find something nice and neutral to occupy our thoughts."

Laughing, he said, "Didn't you write a scene or two for *Varney* today? Bring it on. Nothing like a spot of editing to quell one's ardor."

In the office, they spent over an hour cheerfully dissecting the dialogue she'd composed that afternoon. When Claude delivered her Varney's lines with melodramatic verbal flourishes, exaggerated arm-waving and villainous leers, she collapsed in a fit of giggles. He also offered serious advice for revision, showing that he'd given a lot of thought to how the story should be staged. She could get to like this routine all too quickly. She had to remind herself that her future probably didn't hold nights of passion and literary debates with a ravishing vampire. More likely, Claude's warnings about Philip Trent masked a wish to nudge her out of his life. In reminiscing about his last donor in the 1890s, Claude had made his anxieties about "addiction" clear enough, hadn't he?

They spent the rest of the night watching movies downstairs. Eloise welcomed the immersion in imaginary realms to keep her brain from buzzing with doubt and fear. If she had to turn into a pumpkin at sunrise, at least she could enjoy these few hours. Claude carefully sat at arm's length from her again, but she undercut his caution by reaching across the space between them to capture his hand. He didn't try to retrieve it.

She delighted in making him squirm by tickling the little hairs in his palm. He retaliated by rubbing his thumb over the pulse point on her wrist. Electric currents raced up her arm, made her nipples peak and zinged down to the spot between her legs. She squeezed her thighs in a futile attempt at relief. Knowing he could scent the moisture gathering there, she almost wished he would cuddle up to her and start nibbling again. But he maintained his self-control. Damn.

Dawn came too soon. After the little packing she needed to do, she went to the main floor to find Claude waiting for her in the living room. He clasped her hand and kissed it, a faint brush of his lips on her palm. The contrast between his cool grip and the heat of his mouth made her insides vibrate. "I'd better call a cab for you," he said, "however much I'd rather not."

"I'm already wondering if what I remember from last night really happened." She reclaimed her hand and wrung her fingers together. "When will I see you again?"

"As soon as I think it's safe."

"That's no answer!"

He shrugged. "We can finalize the movie deal and finish the script without meeting face-to-face. After a few weeks have passed, maybe Philip will cool off enough that I can talk to him, make him see reason."

"Meanwhile, I wait around for you to decide my future?"

"Please don't make this so difficult. I want you near me, but I want you alive even more." He reached around to massage the nape of her neck, and she couldn't summon the strength to evade him. "If anything happened to you, I wouldn't jump into a volcano, but my heart would feel charred to ashes."

"You talk a good line. Prove it."

His eyebrows arched. "How?"

"You read my emotions like large print, and yours are a closed book to me. I don't have anything to go on except your word. You say two-way blood sharing creates a telepathic bond, right?"

"That's right." His voice sounded tight with stress.

"So let's do it. Let me drink your blood and read your mind."

Chapter Eleven

e stepped away from her, spread his hands as if in mute appeal and lowered his voice. "Eloise, are you quite sure you want this?"

She planted her clenched fists on her hips. "I don't believe it. You're afraid."

"Cautious, rather. So far, we haven't passed the point of no return for biochemical dependency. If you taste my blood, we'll be locked into a bond that we couldn't break without pain. From what I've been told, pain like gouging one's heart from one's chest."

"Told? You mean you don't know?"

He shook his head. "Not from firsthand experience."

Somehow she'd assumed he had bonded with his previous donor. A thread of satisfaction trickled through her when she realized he hadn't. "Then you've never done this before?"

"'What, never?'" he said with a wry smile. "'No,

never. Well, hardly ever.'" He finished the quote from *H.M.S. Pinafore*. "Only with my adviser, for teaching purposes. I understand bonding with a donor is very different, the most exquisitely intense union one can possibly imagine." Cupping her chin to make her meet his glittering eyes, he said, "Please make sure you choose this freely. Afterward, neither of us will be able to choose with unclouded minds."

She heaved a deep breath. "Yes, I choose. If you're willing, I'm ready."

"If that's what you need to make you trust me, I'm willing." He added with a shaky laugh, "Eager." His arm encircled her waist. "We'd better retire to the bedroom and get comfortable. When we black out from the intensity, we want to be lying down already."

"You're putting me on, aren't you?" she said as they walked upstairs. "Will that really happen?"

"I don't know. We're exploring uncharted territory here. I've heard it can become that powerful though."

In his bedroom, she knelt on the satin sheets to watch him light the vanilla-scented candle and undress in its glow. His pale torso looked like a marble sculpture of a Greek god, animated by magic. Towering over her, he twined his fingers through her hair and clasped her to his chest. The slow beat of his heart thundered in her ears. She couldn't resist flicking her tongue out to tease one of his nipples.

It hardened instantly. Groaning, he convulsively tightened his embrace. Through gritted teeth he said, "Enough." He eased her onto the mattress. "In this condition, my whole body is hypersensitive. If we want to forge the bond, we'd better do it before I forget why we're here." He stripped off her shirt and bra with rapid movements, as if he feared getting distracted. With his help, she wiggled out of the rest of her clothes. "Beautiful." His voice shook.

"You have a vivid imagination."

"When you see yourself through my eyes, you'll understand." He stretched out so that they reclined side by side, facing each other. "Ready?"

She nodded, snuggling closer to him. Her nipples grazed his chest, and his cool thighs pressed against hers. The tip of his quiescent organ brushed the curls on her mound. Warmth spread through her lower abdomen and pooled between her legs.

Claude turned his head to bite his own shoulder. With a hand on the back of her head, he urged her toward the half-inch slash. She hesitantly licked the blood that oozed from it. His body spasmed, his arms tightening around her.

"Yes," he hissed. "Don't stop."

She clamped her mouth onto the wound and sucked. It tasted salty and metallic, like the heated-iron scent of his skin. A low growl thrummed in his throat. No, she thought, more like a purr.

His palms ranged over her back and the curve of her bottom. His teeth pierced her neck. She felt her pulse leap to quench his thirst. His blood effervesced like champagne in her mouth.

She plunged into his mind like diving into a bottomless lake. At the same moment, she felt him flow into all the crevices of her body and brain. She tasted her blood as he swallowed it, like fine sherry. It warmed him all the way to the pit of his stomach and spread through every vein. She felt the way her breasts and thighs seared his skin. She felt the hairs in his palms bristle when they stroked her. The electricity made her own skin tingle.

Merging deeper into his senses, she shared his vision. To

him, she appeared enveloped in a halo of rose-pink and, at the apex of her thighs, turgid red. Surrounding that red haze, she saw a rainbow of coruscating light that radiated from her and undulated with each move she made.

Your aura. Claude's voice in her mind sounded deeper, more resonant, than his normal speech. It reverberated through her insides and made her diaphragm quiver like the surface of a drum. *Now you see how beautiful you are.*

I can hear my own heartbeat. Not only that, through his ears she heard the blood rushing beneath her skin.

In a surge of still deeper immersion, she felt his delight in her amazement. She sensed him watching himself through her eyes and tasting his own blood on her lips as well as hers in his mouth. When his hand crept between their bodies to caress her breasts, she felt the tingle in his palm along with his pleasure in feeling the ache in her taut nipples. She closed her eyes, overwhelmed by the tangle of sensations.

His hand skimmed over her abdomen to the triangle of hair. When he probed for the bud inside that nest, she began to melt instantly.

You're flowing with honey, he silently told her. *And I feel it now, from within. Your wetness, your need.*

Her clit was already twitching. She moaned and rocked her hips toward him.

I know, ma belle. *I share that ache.* His fingers traced spirals around her swollen bud, stroking nearer and nearer to the burning tip. At the moment she felt she would explode if he delayed any longer, he relieved that burning with frenzied caresses that sent her into convulsions that only erupted afresh each time she thought she'd reached the highest possible peak.

She tasted his blood, her blood, felt her tremors of release echoed in his mind, felt his urgency feeding hers, until both of them were sated and had to stop tasting just to breathe.

Excitement still throbbed through her tender parts though. When Claude guided her hand to his groin, she realized why she felt that way.

I've developed an erection, with no direct contact. Fascinating. He rubbed her hand up and down his shaft. *My body mirrors yours. It wants to sheath itself in you.*

As soon as he projected that thought, she craved the same thing. Nudging her to roll facedown, he climbed on top. She melted all over again. He plunged into her from behind, like a panther mating. And like a cat, he fastened his teeth in the nape of her neck. She felt the penetration of his teeth and his cock, along with the intoxication of her blood trickling into his mouth and the hot tightness of her sheath clenching around him. She felt his rod stiffen still harder in an echo of her clit's swelling. When she throbbed in response, his excitement grew fiercer and fed back to her in an ever-expanding spiral.

She screamed in release, and he answered with a roar of ecstasy.

Sometime later, she drifted down to normal awareness. The shadow of his thoughts lingered in the back of her mind, but she remained within her own senses.

"Will it always feel like that?" she said.

He shifted position so that he lay on his back with her cuddled next to him. "We can revive it at will and control the depth of the union. We don't have to lose ourselves." His tone sounded less confident than the words.

"You don't know either, do you?"

"I already admitted this is unexplored territory for me. And I do want to explore again—much further." He disentangled from her embrace. "Do something for me, please. Go out on the balcony."

At her quizzical glance, he gestured toward one set of drapes on the other side of the room. Opening them partway, she found a door onto a balcony identical to the one in her room. Still naked, she stepped outside.

The wind from the ocean made her skin prickle. The early morning sun shed its light on the waves. She felt Claude reaching into her brain and merging his vision with hers.

Incredible! Eloise, I can see through your eyes. I can see the ocean in daylight.

Couldn't you do that anyway?

What I see is a blinding glare. And the colors! To me, colors on the blue end of the spectrum look washed out. No, I've never seen the ocean like this. His gratitude pierced her to the heart. *You show me a whole new world.*

She felt a sudden emptiness, a hollow space at her core. Somehow she knew the feeling originated with Claude. He needed to touch her. She returned to the bed and flowed into his arms. His shields dissolved, layer upon layer, until she felt him invite her into the shadowed cave of his heart. His thoughts showed her a multifaceted crystal of ice that thawed and vaporized at her touch. "*Mon amour*, I'll never stop needing you." He kissed the top of her head. "But I can't keep you, not until you're safe from Philip. You really have to leave."

Drained, purring with languid satisfaction, she couldn't face the idea of putting on her clothes and facing the world yet. "Yeah, right. Soon. Let's just rest awhile first."

He chuckled. "Very well, *ma chérie*. Just a few minutes."

Chapter Twelve

When she swam up to consciousness, her head lay on Claude's shoulder. He felt as cool and still as marble. No breath expanded his ribs. She swept her hand over his chest, while probing the silence of his mind.

Awareness stirred in him. His eyes opened, the now-familiar crimson gleam in their silver depths fixed on her. He gave her a drowsy, catlike smile.

An instant later, the languor he projected flared into alarm, and he sat up. "Oh, damn, look at the time!"

She rolled over to glance at the alarm clock. After six p.m.

"Confound it, you bloody temptress, I never should have let you lull me to sleep."

"Me, lull you? You're the one who goes into hibernation every day."

"Eloise, you have to get away from here. Now." He

stood up and whipped the covers off her. "Suppose Philip's been watching the house all along and started to get impatient? If he decides you've ignored his warning, he might try something more drastic."

"Okay, I get your point." She felt Claude's anxiety beating against her like the wings of a caged hawk. Scooping up her clothes, she went into the bathroom to wash and dress.

When she emerged, Claude had dressed too, though he hadn't bothered to comb his sleep-ruffled hair. "I've phoned a cab. You go up to the road and wait for it. If Philip's around, he'll see you're leaving. Escaping from the evil vampire's clutches."

"Right, but not for long. If we're physically dependent on each other now . . ."

"I more than you. I can't feed on any other human donor. Only you." He rubbed his eyes. "A factor I conveniently overlooked when I agreed to the bond. I can't stay away from you more than a few days."

She threw herself into his arms. His passion and fear for her flowed over her until she thought she might melt into him and drown all over again. She forced herself to slip out of his embrace. "We'll manage somehow. You didn't think I planned to let you stay away anyhow, did you?"

He nodded toward the nightstand. "I suggest you wear that trinket Philip gave you. Displaying an anti-vampire talisman will lend credibility to the ruse."

"Good idea." She hung the cross around her neck. "Here I go, one ruse coming up."

Claude walked her to the foyer but stood well away from the door when she opened it. She marched up the drive to the road, overnight bag and purse slung over her shoulders, briefcase in one hand, trying to project revulsion toward all things vampiric. It didn't work. She had no talent for acting. She settled for blanking her mind so that if Philip spied on her, at least he wouldn't sense her yearning for Claude.

At the edge of the road, she set down her bags and glanced both ways. Claude hadn't mentioned how long the taxi would take to arrive. She blinked in the late afternoon sun. The sea breeze cooled her flushed cheeks. So many things had happened to her since the last time she'd stepped outside in daylight. Now, with her thoughts deliberately blocked from any contact with Claude that might alert his enemy to her true feelings, she couldn't help wondering about the reality of those experiences. Had she dreamed it all? Lost her mind? Succumbed to a complex, brain-twisting form of hypnosis?

She shook her head to dispel the mental fog. Impossible. *More impossible than vampires?* Well, hardly less impossible. What ordinary human being could hypnotize anyone to that extent without the aid of powerful psychotropic drugs? And the theory that Claude had drugged her into accepting such a wild tale and imagining they could read each other's minds struck her as more far-fetched than a race of naturally evolved vampires.

She would see him again in a few nights, no matter how carefully they had to avoid Philip's hypothetical surveillance. They belonged to each other now. She had to hang on to that belief.

From the corner of her eye, she glimpsed the movement of a shadow.

She clutched the cross on its chain around her neck. The shadow oozed toward her. A man in white loomed at her side.

She stumbled backward with a yelp of alarm. Philip grabbed her wrist.

"What do you think you're doing? Let go of me."

He took off his sunglasses. "You stayed here longer than I expected. I became worried about your welfare."

"Well, you can forget it. You warned me to get away, and I'm leaving." With the cross digging into her curled fingers, she remembered Claude's remark about faith in the symbol as a focus for resistance. Maybe it would help her guard against Philip's psychic perception. She concentrated on keeping her mind blank.

"But why didn't you leave much sooner, hmm?" He scraped a fingernail along her jawline.

Eloise shuddered. "My cab will get here any minute. Just let go of me."

"Could it be that my old friend seduced you?"

"I don't know what you're talking about."

He squeezed her wrist painfully hard. "You can't lie to me. I can see through your flimsy shields."

"Let go or I'll scream." She scanned the road. No cars whose drivers might notice if she struggled. No houses in sight, nobody close enough to hear a cry for help.

"No, you won't." Philip's eyes impaled hers. "Be still."

She froze. Inside, she strained against the psychic manacles, but her muscles remained paralyzed.

Philip picked her up and slung her across his shoulder. A whirlwind rushed past her. The landscape went gray before her eyes. A second later, her vision cleared to show a view of the ocean. At her feet she saw emptiness, dropping straight down to the tide line. She stood on a ridge overlooking Claude's private beach. Philip's arm encircled her waist from behind, tightening like a vise when she made a feeble attempt to wiggle free.

"Go ahead and scream now. I want Claude to know I have his pet."

"I'm not his pet," she whispered.

"More than a pet? No?" The soft voice mocked her. "Then he won't mind if I have a taste." The man's tongue circled her earlobe then penetrated the ear.

She trembled, swallowing a spasm of nausea. Yet to her disgust she also felt a faintly erotic flutter in the pit of her stomach.

"Whatever pleasure he can give you, so can I." Philip's teeth rested on the side of her neck, not quite piercing the skin.

Eloise gave up her attempt to maintain the mental barrier. *Claude! I need you!*

His response crashed like a tidal wave against her barrier, flattening it instantly. *Eloise?* She felt him rush toward her.

Seconds after she called, Philip half-turned, still gripping her around the waist. "Claude. Stop there." The nails of his free hand dug into the skin of Eloise's neck.

She saw Claude standing about ten feet away. Unlike Philip, he wore short sleeves and no hat. This early in the evening, the sun still glared on his unprotected skin and eyes. She sensed his incipient headache and the way the light scorched his arms. Those discomforts faded to the background though. His fear for her dominated his thoughts.

"Philip, old thing, you don't need to do this. I admit I treated you shabbily. You have a perfect right to your anger. But Eloise has nothing to do with that."

"Of course she does. You destroyed my favorite—my beloved. I'm taking yours."

"What makes you think she's my favorite, much less 'beloved'? That's a human emotion."

Eloise reached for Claude's mind and hit a blank wall. She assured herself he probably had his shield up to keep the attacker from reading him. Yet she couldn't tame the fear that he displayed no emotions because he didn't feel any. Because all the passion and need she remembered had been nothing but an illusion to add spice to the feast.

Philip edged to the very rim of the cliff and leaned so that she momentarily tilted outward above the drop. Her stomach churned. Head spinning, she clung to the arm locked around her waist. A shaft of alarm from Claude stabbed her.

With a cold chuckle, Philip straightened up. "What a disgraceful lack of control, Claude. You broadcast that reaction like a beacon from a lighthouse. Now tell me you don't feel anything for this pet."

"Only what I'd feel if you endangered any ephemeral for pure vengeance. I bitterly regret the death of your donor. I don't want to see anyone else die for my negligence."

"Is that an apology? And a plea, no less?"

"Take it as whatever you'd like." Claude glided a pace or two nearer, stopping when Philip clawed Eloise's neck once more. "I'll apologize all you want. Hell, I'll grovel. Just let her go and face me like a man of honor."

"Now you're talking in human terms. Since when does a vampire's honor depend on an ephemeral's welfare? At least according to you. I could always find another pet, you said."

Eloise felt the anger boiling under the surface of Claude's mind. "Damn it, I said I was wrong."

"You think a simple apology makes up for her death and all the years I lost?"

"What more do you expect? I can't bring your donor back."

Philip licked Eloise's ear again. His tongue felt the way she imagined a snake's forked tongue might. Fear swamped any trace of arousal. "I'll take this one as a substitute," he said.

Claude bared his teeth. "Not a chance." His hands curled like talons.

"Fascinating. You're in love with this woman."

"Don't be absurd." The chill in his voice sounded almost genuine enough to confirm that she had fantasized those hours of passion they'd shared.

A growl rumbled in Philip's chest. "You know we can't lie to each other. I can see the strength of your feeling for her."

"We used to be friends. I don't want to kill you."

"You'd make yourself an outcast for an ephemeral? Better and better." He nipped the side of her neck.

She felt the trickle of blood and the flick of his tongue. He didn't continue feeding though. He obviously intended the violation just to taunt Claude. To underscore the message, he grazed her breast with his free hand.

Claude stood motionless, staring at the two on the edge of the cliff. He spoke inside Eloise's mind: *I don't dare charge. He could tear your throat out before I got anywhere near you.* His thoughts lay bare to her. She saw a vision of herself lying on the ground with blood fountaining from a fatal wound and felt his near panic at the image.

Then what do we do?

The reply came as an unexpected shock: *You have to make him drop you.*

Her stomach lurched. *What?*

Rather, you have to make him let go long enough for you to jump off the edge.

Are you nuts?

Claude's mental voice thrummed with tension. *It's the only way. I can catch you before you hit the ground. He won't be expecting that.*

He expected her to believe he could cover the distance faster than she could fall? She went lightheaded at the mere thought. *I don't think I can make myself do it.*

It's our only reasonable chance. Eloise, please, you have to trust me.

Trust a man who wasn't even human? Letting him feast on her blood and ravish her body and mind was one thing, but this—! Trusting him too far in this case could have a fatal result.

On the other hand, so could not trusting. The wet suction of Philip's mouth tugged at her throat. At any moment, he might decide to sink his teeth in, just to watch Claude's reaction.

All right, she silently answered. *I'll try.*

Make her captor let go? How? What did she know about a vampire's vulnerability? Too bad Philip didn't suffer from a religious phobia. The cross wouldn't work as a weapon. What about physiological weaknesses all his kind shared? She rummaged in her memories of the nights with Claude. One "weakness" came to mind, the way he'd practically whimpered when she'd tickled his palms.

Philip had one hand within easy reach, loosely cupping her breast. She insinuated her own hand between his arm and her body. At the same time, she went limp, hoping to make him think she'd given up resisting. Her fingertips brushed the fine hairs in his palm. He growled into her neck, looked up and said to Claude, "Ah, she likes it. You see, any vampire can please her. You're wasting energy to concern yourself with this woman." He returned his mouth to the minute wound.

Swallowing her revulsion, she stroked the hairs in a light spiral pattern. He moaned with evident pleasure. She leaned into his arm, toward the cliff's edge.

Now, Eloise, Claude urged. *I'm ready.*

While she mechanically kept up her fake seduction, her brain screamed, *I can't do this, I just can't!*

Then let me help you. I promised not to override your will, but if you give me permission, I can make you jump.

Let him take over her mind and body? Operate her like a puppet? Still, if she didn't have faith that he would release his control the instant after he caught her, she might as well admit she didn't trust him at all. *Fine! Do it!*

She dug her nails into Philip's palm and gouged the most sensitive spot. With a howl of pain and rage, he momentarily spasmed and relaxed his grip. She mentally reached for Claude and felt his will wrap her mind like a spider's silk. He slipped inside her nerves and muscles like a man putting on a cloak.

Her body launched itself into the void. The surf on the rocks rushed toward her. Her head reeled, and her stomach turned inside out. A scream ripped from her throat.

Chapter Thirteen

 blur of motion swooped under her. She landed in Claude's arms. He sprinted down the beach and halted in a swirl of sand.

Shaking, but with her feet on the ground, she clung to him. Her head spun as if she had just crawled out of a roller coaster car.

"It's all right, *chérie*." His hands stroked her head and her back. "I have to leave you for a minute. Stay here."

Like I can do anything else? When he let go of her, she collapsed onto the sand. She watched him levitate up to the ridge toward Philip, who crouched there roaring in fury.

Claude charged at the other vampire and slammed him to the ground. Philip rammed a fist into Claude's face and broke his hold. Through the blood-bond, Eloise's nerves echoed the pain of the blow. The two men rolled over, Claude underneath now. He rallied instantly, shoved his opponent off and flipped him onto his back.

Though the pounding of the waves made it hard for Eloise to hear the next few words, she picked up the conversation through Claude's mind.

"Talk about wasting energy, old man. Don't bother struggling. I'm stronger than you are. You probably haven't fed worth a damn in the past few nights, with all your time spent stalking Eloise. I've feasted well." He punctuated the sentence with a hard slap to the other man's face.

"Go ahead and kill me," came Philip's sullen response. "I detest what this world has become. Noisy, artificial, foul-smelling—"

"I said I didn't want to kill you. But I'm sure as hell not going to let you run loose. Perhaps another long stretch of undeath will help you see reason."

"In other words, you plan to kill me temporarily." The other vampire's weary voice held a sardonic edge.

"Call it whatever you wish. The point is to make Eloise safe from you." Claude wrapped his hands around Philip's neck.

"Fine. At least I got to see you besotted with an ephemeral. When you thought I might slaughter your woman, you were terrified. That's satisfaction enough."

Claude tightened his grip until Philip stopped breathing and his body went slack. Through Claude's ears, Eloise heard the other vampire's heart fall silent. *Is he dead?*

Only dormant. And I'll make sure he stays that way for the foreseeable future. Picking up the body, Claude sprang off the ridge and hovered above the ocean surface. He raised the body over his head. With a strength she couldn't have imagined, he heaved the inert form offshore, the distance of a couple of football fields. It sank instantly.

Claude floated down to her side, helped her stand up and

folded her in a tight embrace. "He won't drown, but he won't wake up either. Not as long as he stays underwater."

"He'll wash ashore, though, won't he?"

Leading her toward the stairs that ascended to the patio, he said, "Not any time soon. You see, he's not dead, so his body won't float like a corpse. On the other hand, let's hope for his sake the local sea life doesn't find vampire flesh appetizing."

Her stomach knotted.

"Forgive me for subjecting you to all this."

She swallowed. "It's Philip's fault, not yours."

"I'll report to the elders and ask their advice. Eventually, I may have to dredge him up and revive him myself. When and if I feel sure I can keep him away from you."

She edged away from Claude, her fingers groping for the crucifix around her neck. "But you almost killed him . . ."

"Oh, damn. Please don't fear me." His hand rested lightly on her arm. "I bear no malice toward the poor blighter. Now I know how he felt when his lady died. The same way I'd feel if I lost you." He opened his mind and showed her a bleak expanse of desert baking under a remorseless sun. He glanced briefly at the cross. "You said you believe I'm not a demon, that your Deity made my kind for a purpose."

She clutched the crucifix like an anchor. "I do believe that. I know you're not evil." Slowly, her grasp relaxed, and she unhooked the silver chain.

"I'm not asking you to forsake your religion," he said. "Only that it not make a barrier between us."

"It won't." She tucked the cross into her pants pocket and allowed Claude to put his arm around her waist.

He helped her into the den and settled her on the couch. "It's a relief to get out of the sun. I need a drink of water. Let me bring you one too." When he returned with two glasses of ice water, he said, "I wouldn't blame you if you wanted to leave anyhow, right this minute. Your choice. Needless to say, whatever you do won't affect our movie deal."

She took a long gulp of the water. Her stomach began to calm down. "Good grief, I forgot all about the cab. He probably came and went already."

"I can drive you to the airport myself if you like." He sat on the edge of the couch, at arm's length from her. She felt the uncertainty preying on his mind.

Uncertainty of what? Her feelings or his own?

"That depends," she said, staring into her glass.

"On what?"

"What Philip said." She forced the words past a lump in her throat. "That vampires can't lie to each other."

"No, the most we can do is conceal our emotions, not disguise them."

"He also said you're in love with me. Well?"

The surface of Claude's mind churned like a windswept lake. "If he saw that in my aura, it must be true."

Moisture blurred her vision. "Again with the non-answer."

"*Chérie*, I don't know how to answer. I have never experienced an emotion like this before. As if you've already grown roots into my heart." His eyes widened. "Oh, hell. Poetic justice at its best. I'm not just addicted. I *am* in love with you."

"Do you have to sound like it's a fate worse than death?" Her voice rasped with suppressed tears.

"Not that. But still terribly strange. I. Love. You." He moved next to her, clasped her hand and kissed it. Sparks danced up her arm and over her entire body. She felt the same electricity sizzling through him. "Eloise, our bond gives me access to your deepest thoughts and desires. But it doesn't analyze and define them. You have to tell me in words. Do you love me?"

Trembling, she let her hand rest in his while she considered. "You threatened to make yourself an outcast by destroying Philip for me. You guided me to escape from him and then released control instantly, the way you promised. You could mesmerize me into any emotion you want me to feel, but you're not." She laid her free hand on his chest, and he shivered, his eyes half-closed. "I love you, Claude."

With a groan, he drew her into a tight embrace. She twisted around, trying to press her body against his. She ended up in his lap, her head on his shoulder.

"Stay with me. Marry me."

She insinuated her hand into his shirt and heard a purr in his throat when she skimmed her nails over his chest. "Marry? That's so human of you."

He nipped her earlobe without piercing the skin. "Human? Please, no insults. *Mon amour*, I promise not to treat you like a pet. Keep your own home, if you need a refuge sometimes. And, of course, your own work and bank account. I want marriage under your laws though. I'll have no lurid supermarket tabloid speculation about you. I want the world to know you belong to me. Legally and permanently."

"As long as you know it works both ways. You belong to me too."

"*Certainement.* That's what the blood-bond means." He hugged her so tightly she had to gasp for breath. "You hold my life in your hands, forever. We possess each other as long as our hearts beat."

Tracing a scratch on his collarbone with a fingernail, he guided her lips to the wound. His mouth fastened on her neck, and the life-force flowed between them in an unbroken circle. Their hearts pulsed in unison. Like two rivers pouring into one sea, their blood and passion merged. Forever.

Curse of
Brandon Lupinus

✦

SHELLEY MUNRO

Chapter One

Y ou're the new owner of Tavistock Manor." The elderly lady who approached Jess's table carried a cane and appeared frail, but her eyes were full of curious intelligence.

Jess Whittlebury held back a smile, aware she'd been under observation from the moment she'd strolled the cobblestone street with its quaint bow-window shops and entered the Brass Kettle Tea Shop. She'd made a silent bet with herself as to how long it would take one of the elderly women to approach. Jess set her teacup down in the duck-egg blue china saucer. She leaned back in her wooden chair and nodded at the woman across the vase of fresh flowers. "Yes, I'm Jess Whittlebury."

"I hear you're turning the manor into a bed and break-fast," the tiny gray-haired woman said. In her peripheral vision Jess noticed the other women craning their necks, ears practically flapping with eagerness to hear the conversation.

"That's right," Jess said, and to appease their curiosity she added, "I fell in love with the manor when I drove up the winding road and glimpsed it amongst the oak trees. The medieval church and narrow streets of the village remind me of the town where I grew up in Yorkshire. I've purchased my own slice of heaven."

The lady leaned closer in a confidential manner. "You know it's haunted."

Her audience seemed to hold a collective breath. Jess stifled her amusement. The real estate agent had informed her of the manor's extra resident, but that only increased the potential for her bed and breakfast. American tourists loved history, and a spooky ghost story added pounds onto her investment.

"I've heard."

"The ghost is real. On a clear night you can hear him howling."

"The werewolf," Jess said. "I wonder why he does that?"

The elderly woman snorted. "Romantics say he pines for his true love. I think he's tired of being alone. You should watch yourself, Miss Jess. Our local legends are full of werewolf tales. There's always an element of truth in myth and legend."

Another woman ambled up to Jess's table, slow because of the excess weight she carried. "These days it's not safe for a body to live or walk alone. Megan Dean, the schoolmaster's daughter, was attacked and robbed last week. They say if the landscaper hadn't driven past and scared them off, it could have been much worse."

"Tish-tosh," the first lady said in a chiding manner. "Don't scare Miss Jess. I'm sure her bed and breakfast will provide lots of visitors to the village. Besides, a ghost werewolf is better than an alarm or guard dog."

"True enough, Hilda." The second lady nodded. "It's good to have new blood. We don't want our village to die like Martindale."

Jess smiled and picked up the china teapot to refresh her cup. She added another slice of lemon and took a sip. Talk of ghosts didn't dampen her excitement. Jess Whittlebury was in pursuit of a dream. A little physical work to tame the overgrown garden and some repairs and remodeling inside were all that was required. Thanks to her father and brother, she had the skills to complete most of the work on her own. In about three months she'd open for the start of the summer season.

Jess worked in the garden for most of the afternoon, rescuing roses from suffocation. A cool breeze lashed her cheeks and tugged at her heavy coat but she continued yanking the weeds and digging out clumps of grass that choked the original garden beds. With winter still grasping the countryside, she needed to take advantage of the days it didn't rain or, worse, snow. Luckily, the winter had been mild and the snow had disappeared over a month ago. She hoped the mild weather continued.

Finally when it was too dark to see more than her hand in front of her face, she stood and flexed her aching shoulders. Jess collected her spade and headed for the house.

Without warning, the wail of the wind ceased and the mournful cry of a wolf resounded through the valley. Jess gasped, her heart drumming against her ribs. The hairs at the back of her neck bristled and she scarcely breathed until the final echoes died. A second howl followed. Jess swallowed before common sense told her it was local teenagers trying to scare off the newcomer. While she was glad of the legend attached to her property, she didn't believe in ghosts or were-wolves. They were the romantic fancies of novelists.

Jess laughed softly and continued up the uneven path to the side of the house where a former owner had attached a garage. She stowed her spade in the garage and continued along the narrow path to the front door. A sense of pride filled her when she paused at the entrance and pictured a profusion of blooms filling the weed-choked gardens. The L-shaped medieval manor had gone through renovations during the years and bore traces of Georgian and Victorian owners as well as modern atrocities such as purple paint. Built of golden Cotswold stone, Jess imagined the manor would glow like warm honey during the summer when it was bathed in sunlight. The manor had real character.

She opened the heavy wooden door and let herself into the vestibule. The ceilings were high and the rooms spacious. Although the walls were rough at the moment with strips of peeling wallpaper and ugly paint, there was potential. That was good enough for Jess.

A third howl made her pause before she shrugged out of her coat, tugged off her woolen hat and pulled off the protective gardening gloves. She shut the door half amused at the teenagers' prank then hung her garments on the coatrack in the corner to her right. Supernatural beasties. Huh!

Jess followed the hall to the end and stepped into the kitchen. First a quick meal of soup and toast, then she intended to start stripping the wallpaper in the parlor. Summer was fast approaching and there was no time to waste.

Brandon Lupinus lifted his shaggy black head and howled. A sense of surprise filled him at the urge to shift to wolf when the full moon was still a week away. The sound, pure and eerie, rippled from his ghostly throat sending exhilaration through Brandon. Before the last echoes died he padded down the hill into the valley below. Wind shook the skeleton branches and sent the dead leaves skittering across the ground. Mist swirled around him as he headed unerringly toward the manor.

The scent of rich, freshly turned soil along with cut foliage filled the air when he trotted past the gardens in the front of the manor. On reaching the door, he passed through the thick wood without breaking stride. Once inside, he shifted to his human form. Dressed in black breeches, a white shirt with lace on the sleeves and a black and red embroidered waistcoat, he appeared the epitome of the eighteenth-century gentleman.

Brandon drifted up the stairs, excitement building inside him. Curiosity. Another owner for his country estate. Mostly, he didn't care. He'd lost count of the owners over the years, but he'd never felt this burgeoning anticipation before. At the top of the stairs he turned left toward the main chambers. The doors stood open and the stench of paint offended his nose. The woman was changing the interior. Again. Not that it made much difference with the hodgepodge of styles inflicted by previous owners, including his father. She would leave and another would come. He eased through the walls of each chamber without impediment, taking in her progress before returning to the passageway.

The woman's presence filled the air with energy. It sizzled through his body, drawing him in. Heady. Intoxicating. Unheard of and unnerving. Brandon paused outside the stout oak door leading to the master bedroom. His heart thumped. He swallowed and felt the muscles in his throat contract. He . . . felt. After hundreds of years walking alone, cursed by the old witch, he felt something other than cold, other than ice. Strange. Perhaps it was an age thing and he was gaining power. Or not. The words of the curse echoed through his mind. *Walk the ghostly world. Howl at the moon. Alone, Brandon Lupinus, until need forces you to act as a decent man should.*

He had puzzled over the meaning, walking the ghostly void alone ever since the words had passed the witch's lips. Neither wolf nor ghost but a mixture, forced to live in solitary while his father passed through the heavenly gates to live in peaceful paradise.

A small cry jerked him from memories. Brandon burst through the wooden door, curiosity and a trace of fear for the woman lending him speed. One look told him it was naught but a dream causing her to cry out. He drifted up to the four-poster bed and gazed down at her sleep-flushed face. Her dark brown hair was cut short like a lad's. Her face was browned from the sun yet it, along with the tiny sun-kissed spots on her face, gave her a pixieish charm. A man would want to touch each of the speckles with his mouth. Explore. Brandon reached out to brush ghostly fingers across her cheekbone, wishing more than anything to feel the silky skin of a woman again. Just once. His chest lifted and fell in a ghostly sigh. Impossible since ghosts didn't feel anything but cold. He lowered his fingers anyway, delicately brushing a tiny freckle. A flare of warmth burst up his arm without warning. Instead of the expected chill, he savored the heat from her skin. She made a soft mewing sound and flung up her arm, hitting his shoulder before it passed through him.

By God's teeth! He'd felt that too. Astonished, he stared at the woman. She'd dislodged the covers and he could see her tanned throat and chest. The scanty covering she wore hid nothing of her upper body, clinging in a way that made him sigh again. Elsa . . . Brandon cursed under his breath. Aye, stupidity that had been and now he paid the price.

The woman moaned in her sleep, giving a robust kick strong enough to send the covers sliding off the edge of the bed. Brandon couldn't help but stare. Her breasts were large and round, her rosy nipples visible through the pink cloth that barely covered her chest. Her long legs were clothed in a darker pink cloth, her limbs clearly visible. Brandon watched her carefully lest she woke. There! He felt it again. Energy arcing between them.

His gaze moved to her breasts and lingered, the urge to touch again so strong he was powerless to resist. His big hand trembled when he reached out. Lightly, he cupped one full breast. A hiss emerged as the warmth of her skin permeated him. He couldn't have moved if he tried. Brandon brushed his thumb across the tip of her nipple. Once. Twice. A third time. In fascination, he watched the rosy nipple contract to a hard nub. His body reacted with a mighty surge of power. The heat emanating from her body filled him, sending shimmering feeling shooting the length of his body. His cock firmed and lengthened. His ghostly heart thumped as it never had before. Brandon's other senses kicked in. Smell. God's teeth, her scent was intoxicating. Clean woman. Soap. He leaned toward her breasts, inhaling deeply. Joy bubbled through him at this unexpected gift. Taste. Could he taste? Dare he? He was so close. Willing the woman to remain asleep, he huffed a breath on her contracted nipple. Even beneath the barrier of cloth, she responded to his touch, to him. His cock tightened even more. Slowly he opened his mouth and took the tender tip between his lips. Yes! He tasted the furriness of the cloth and smelled her soapy scent. His tongue darted out to tease and touch while his lips clasped the woman's nipple. Ah, but she tasted sweet. He applied a hint of teeth and she moaned. Brandon froze in alarm until she splayed her legs and whimpered. So responsive. He had barely touched her. Emboldened, he drew on her nipple and palmed the other with his hand. Soft, yielding flesh. What would it be like to touch her skin without the barrier of the cloth?

Brandon inhaled deeply, the myriad sensations pounding through his body threatening to unman him. For so long he'd focused on breaking the curse, yet nothing worked to solve the witch's riddle. Sex. Hell, he hadn't even thought of sex in over two hundred years, but now he felt the lack. His cock ached something fierce, his balls drawn up tight from merely sucking on the woman's breast like a babe. God's teeth, he hungered for more—the warm glove of her pussy clinging to his manhood. He desperately wanted her holding him, clutching at his shoulders and digging her fingernails into his back when she came. Brandon shuddered, his chest rising and falling beneath his shirt and vest. His breeches were an encumbrance, no longer fitting to his lower body but tight like a vise. Brandon willed his clothing away and drifted from his feet until he hovered naked above her semi-clad body. *Please don't wake up, sweetheart. Let me love you.*

Slowly, he sank downward until her luscious curves melded to his chest. He had substance. He could feel. And taste. He could touch. Tears formed at the corners of his eyes, prickling uncomfortably against the need to stay strong. Oh she felt so good, her legs spread for him to lie between. Greedily, he wanted more. Brandon held his breath and slipped his hand beneath the pink cloth to touch the warm skin beneath.

Silky. Soft and fragrant. His hand crept upward to cup her breast again. Brandon shuddered at the exquisite sensation of her skin beneath the calloused pads of his fingers. The woman arched her body upward as if seeking more from him. Brandon was happy to oblige. Gently he tugged the cloth up over her breasts. The woman smiled in her sleep and raised her hands over her head to aid him in the task. Finally she was naked from the waist upward and he could look his fill.

Her pink nipples were hard points designed to draw his attention. He swallowed, wishing to savor her treasures. A soft murmur escaped her lips, demanding almost. Brandon bent his head and licked a path from the plump base of her breast all the way to the tip. He suckled at his leisure, loving the way she undulated against his tight loins. Teasing him. Asking for him to give more. Brandon rose to hover above her again. He removed the pink trews, peeling them down long, slender legs. He had to taste her intimately while his senses were receptive. Her legs parted automatically for him, the scent of her arousal filling the air.

For him.

Brandon was so full of joy he wanted to throw back his head and howl. Time for that later when the danger of waking her had passed. He kissed a trail from her breast downward, determined to go slow despite the risk. It made his hunger sharper when balanced on a sword's edge like this. His heart pounded, the fullness of his cock urging him to speed. Brandon knew he would spill his seed quickly once he entered her tight warmth, but his pleasure would increase tenfold if she enjoyed the loving too. He stroked his fingers across her ribs, watching her expression the entire time. She smiled, wriggling slightly as if she were ticklish. Brandon's hand trailed lower, across her abdomen, stopping a fraction above the dark curls that guarded her femininity. He moved down the mattress and between her legs so his face was level with her pussy. Inhaling deeply, he savored her musky scent. His fingers trailed lower, skimming across her folds and dipping into moist heat. She shifted, raising her hips into his touch. A lover who knew what she wanted, one who wasn't afraid to communicate her needs. Brandon knew he was a lucky man. *Ghost.* The correction sobered him for an instant but each of his senses continued to clamor for more. Brandon didn't think he could stop now if he tried.

Jess tossed her head from side to side, feeling as though she were poised on the edge of a precipice. Her body tingled insistently. Her breasts ached from her dream lover sucking and teasing them with his teeth. Fiery heat blazed between her legs. Her lover parted her swollen folds and lowered his dark head. The moment his tongue dragged down her cleft she burned for him. The friction of his stubble against the tender skin of her inner thighs was exquisite—a jolt of sharpness to contrast the lazy sweep of his tongue.

Jess arched upward seeking more pressure. A masculine chuckle made her smile. His image danced through her mind. Tall. Solid and muscular with dark hair and flashing come-to-bed gray eyes. His tongue raked the length of her cleft again, sending lightning showers of sparks along her quivering nerves.

"God's teeth, you taste good," he murmured in a husky voice.

And—wow!—he made her feel alive. Jess lifted her hips, rotating slightly to gain pressure where she needed it. "Oh

yes," she whispered at the long echo of sensation that raced
through her. That felt *gooood*. He cupped her butt with his
capable hands, lifting her hips to gain easier access. He drew
out every touch, every lick, lingering and teasing until tension
coiled her body tight.

"Touch me. Please." More begging words backed up in her
throat but he merely chuckled and continued with slow, delib-
erate flicks of his tongue against her clit. His warm breath and
the brush of his tongue worked magic. Slowly the sensation
built, layer upon layer, until the teasing gave way to promise.
His tongue darted into the mouth of her pussy, lapping delicately while his finger stroked her swollen nub. Jess held her
breath as she climbed toward climax. The tingles grew until
suddenly with one last brush of his thumb she shattered. A
series of waves pulsed deep in her cunt, going on and on for
long, endless seconds.

"Yes," she whispered, her voice low and throaty. Sexy.
Damn, but she felt sexy and feminine after her orgasm. The
only thing that would make it better would be his cock
planted deep in her womb. As if he could read her mind, he
moved over her body. He took her mouth in a rough kiss, his
tongue darting between her lips. He tasted of spices, mysteri-
ous and male, and a hint of her juices. Jess moaned, his weight
on top of her body welcome. And very real for a dream. Smiling at the thought of dreaming in color—'cause this dream
was definitely in color—she wound her arms around his neck
and clutched his powerful shoulders. His skin was cool to the
touch. Smooth.

"I need you inside me," she whispered against his neck.
"Now."

"That can be arranged," he murmured in his husky voice.

He drew back, guiding his cock to the mouth of her pussy, then surged into her with one seamless thrust. Her lover was a large man and at first she struggled with his invasion despite her arousal. Luckily, he seemed to sense her trepidation with his size because he stilled, allowing her body to adjust. He took her mouth, gently biting her lips and soothing the sensual stings with his tongue, tasting and tormenting her. Excitement exploded in Jess, bringing a surge of juices to her pussy. Panting, she gasped at the jump in arousal that threatened to burn her from the inside out. She needed him to move, but he seemed content with kisses.

Impatient now, Jess decided to hurry him along. She contracted her inner muscles, clamping down hard on his cock to get his attention. His groan brought a grin of success until he started to move. Jess bit back her answering moan, his hard thrusts hitting her right where she needed him most. She arched her back, shuddering helplessly with each smooth plunge of his cock. A rough growl vibrated in his chest as a haze of hot pleasure swept her away. He thrust frantically for four strokes then stilled, giving out a heartfelt groan that told Jess his climax was as good as her second. She felt the spurt of his seed deep in her womb while his heart drummed against her chest. Wrapping her arms around him, she held tight, enjoying the sense of fulfillment and closeness to her dream lover.

"Thank you," he murmured, his husky voice rich with emotion.

"My pleasure," Jess purred.

He moved off her, separating their bodies. Instantly, Jess mourned the loss and let out a choked protest. A chuckle filled the room as he dragged her into his arms, spooning his body around hers. He kissed her shoulder and whispered, "Sleep, sweetheart."

Jess smiled, her eyelids fluttering. Silly man. She was already asleep. Sex wasn't like that in real life. It wasn't mind-blowing climaxes or two orgasms in one session. It wasn't a hunky man with dark hair longer than her own. It wasn't a man with muscles in the right places instead of ones that had sunk to the gut. Sex was . . . well, boring. She could take it or leave it.

Chapter Two

randon peeled himself away from her warm body, something akin to shock filling his soul. Absently, he flicked his wrist and clothes formed on his body as he tried to make sense of the ball of confusion inside.

The woman.

It had to be the woman.

Brandon forced himself to move away from the four-poster bed before he succumbed to the urge to join her again. He'd enjoyed every part of that loving, experienced it with his newly awakened senses of touch and taste. He tore his gaze off her curvy body and drifted across the Oriental carpet until he reached the bare wooden floor by the door. Brandon passed through the chamber door, a dull pain and tearing sensation throughout his body making him leap out the other side in a panic. What the hell? He raised his hand up in front of his face. God's teeth, he couldn't see through

it! Confusion nipped at him as he strode down the curved staircase to the lower floor. *Strode*. Instead of his usual drift. Hope
bloomed deep in his chest and he sprinted along the hall to the
front door, his boots clunking with each hasty step. Noise. He
was making sounds other than ghostly howls.

When he burst through the stout oak door dull pain assailed
him again. Grinning, Brandon vanquished his clothes and
shifted smoothly all in one move. The discomfort of shifting
burst upon him then—the lengthening of bones and reshap-
ing of jaw and teeth. Brandon dropped to the chilly ground on
all fours and trotted across the damp grass toward the woods
of oak and beech that bordered the rear of the manor estate. An
almost full moon hung in the sky shedding patches of light in
the places where there was no mist. Brandon's breath steamed
from him in a white cloud while dead leaves crackled beneath
his paws. He felt the wind ripple across his fur and gloried at
the sensation. Increasing his pace to a lope, he leapt over a low
stone fence, trotted through the brook at the rear of the manor
and into the trees.

It had to be the woman.

Following a narrow path forged by deer, he headed directly
for the still pond deep in the middle of the woods. He burst
into the clearing, startling a badger. The black and white creature thundered away in panic, but it needn't have worried.
Brandon had more pressing concerns.

The moon struck the pond, giving enough light to show
Brandon what he needed to know. He had a shadow. He had
substance. He had form. With a canine grin, he backed away
from the water and leapt atop a grassy knoll. Throwing back
his head, he let out a howl of pure joy.

It was the woman. Somehow, she'd given him substance.

.   .   .

Shards of early morning light sneaked through the moth holes in the green velvet curtains. One hit Jess in the face and she gave a sleepy murmur of protest. Time to rise and shine. Screwing her eyes tightly shut, she pushed up to a sitting position and swung her legs over the edge of the bed. Raising her arms above her head, Jess stretched leisurely then stood. Her eyes flew open and she glanced down at her naked body in consternation. Fragments of an explicit dream flooded her mind and a flush swept the length of her body. Oh boy. That had been a doozy of a dream if she'd climbed so far into it she'd stripped off her pajamas. A faint whiff of arousal came from her body. The heat in her face intensified before she shrugged and laughed. That was her kind of dream. Bring it on tonight.

Jess washed rapidly in the chilly en suite a previous owner had installed, practically jumping in and out of the shower. Between her legs she was tender, as if she truly had been vigorously loved. Way peculiar. She obviously needed to break her sexual drought the second the opportunity presented itself. Jess swiped a towel over her body and padded back to her bedroom. After retrieving clothes from a heavy mahogany dresser, she pulled on underwear, worn jeans, a Loch Ness monster T-shirt and a woolen sweater. Once her bare feet were clothed in socks, she made her way to the kitchen. A glance out the window confirmed the day was sunny and brisk. Gardening this morning and wallpapering in the parlor this afternoon. After dinner, she'd clear the library of dust and cobwebs and decide which books she'd keep for her guests' amusement.

.   .   .

Brandon watched the woman for most of the day, content to lie beneath a gooseberry bush during the morning, enjoying the heat of the sun in his wolf form. When she returned indoors, he shifted and slipped through the closed door, albeit painfully, to tiptoe after her. After hours of studying her at work, he was filled with admiration. She worked hard without appearing to tire. The woman was large and solid compared to the females of his time. A wide smile bloomed. But not overweight as he knew from his intimate explorations last night. She was much taller, almost as tall as he, a fact Brandon liked since he wouldn't suffer from a crick in his neck when he kissed her. Not that it mattered when a couple was horizontal, but he enjoyed variety when it came to sex. Indoors. Outdoors. Standing. Sitting. Reclining. Yes, variety was good.

His thoughts shifted to his new status. Although his body was less transparent, the woman didn't appear to notice or sense his presence. The curse wasn't broken but maybe a trifle bent? He hoped so. It was when they'd made love that the changes in his transparency and ease of communication had occurred. Brandon stood and wandered across to where the woman squatted, removing books from his bookcase and stacking them neatly in boxes after dusting them with enough vigor to send dust motes dancing through the air. His nose wrinkled when dust billowed in his face. It wouldn't do to sneeze and scare the woman. Brandon wished he knew her name. A quick search of paperwork had only yielded an envelope bearing the name J. Whittlebury, which didn't tell him much. Tonight. Ah tonight, he'd ask before he thrust into her tight pussy and he'd come with her name on his lips.

Brandon shuddered, his cock reacting to his licentious thoughts. He glanced out the window at the rapidly approach-

ing dusk. Already the shrubs were mere shadows against the
darkening sky.

The woman paused to rotate her shoulders and pressed
her hands to the small of her back. She checked the timepiece
on her wrist before continuing to remove the last of the books
from the shelves.

Brandon stepped closer and blew a stream of air over the
tender skin of her neck. To his disappointment, she didn't
react. But all was not lost. Her scent enveloped him—a mixture of green leaves from her work in the garden and a hint of
citrus from the soap she used to cleanse her body. Delectable.
In another test, he tugged on an errant curl. She jerked her
head, pulling her hair from between his fingers. Grinning, he
did it again. This time she slapped at her head as if an insect
troubled her. Her hand went right through his wrist and sent
a jolt of desire coursing straight to his balls. The air whistled
through his teeth. God's teeth, that was unexpected.

He swept his hand over the placket of his breeches, his
touch intensifying the burning arousal that assailed him.
Brandon longed to take her in his arms and kiss her thoroughly. The need to strip off the ugly boy clothes she wore
and bare her silken limbs was almost too much for him. His
hands fisted at his sides and he swore. Bloody curse. Brandon
stalked away from the woman and away from temptation. Gut
instinct told him he needed to wait.

"Who's there?"

Brandon halted immediately, turning slowly to watch the
woman. She was staring directly at him.

"I don't believe in ghosts so stop your stupid tricks. Come
out and show yourself. Now! Before I call the police." Her
voice remained steady but Brandon caught the faint tremor

of her hands. Hell, he hadn't meant to frighten her. At least she hadn't screamed. Elsa had screamed when his friends had taken her against her will. He had laughed until he'd realized it wasn't a game and she truly didn't want sex. It had been too late to stop them breaking her nose and strangling her to death. Dammit, he wished he'd tried harder. For Elsa's sake.

"Please leave."

Brandon cleared his throat, uncertainty making him hesitate. "I wish I could leave."

She frowned and strode around the corner of the huge mahogany desk. The woman marched straight through him without pause, hurrying from the library.

When he could finally breathe through the storm of sensation that held him in thrall, Brandon went after her, his cock still pulsing insistently against his breeches. Hell, the woman packed a sensual punch. He couldn't wait to have her again. Brandon hoped he hadn't frightened her too much.

Jess checked all the windows and doors before her pulse rate settled back to normal. Everything was shut tight. Yet she could have sworn she'd heard footsteps. Sighing, Jess returned to the library to finish packing up the last of the books from the shelves before she prepped the room for a coat of paint. She walked across the dusty Oriental carpet and decided to move the desk and roll up the carpet. The mahogany desk appeared solid. Jess hoped she could shift it on her own. She cleared a path and grabbed the end that housed a set of drawers. To her surprise it slid across the carpet and onto the wooden floor with ease. Jess frowned once the desk was in its new position. It was almost as if someone had taken the other end and pushed. Shoving aside her fanciful thoughts, Jess rolled up the carpet and stowed it against the wall that consisted solely of bookshelves. A glance at her watch told her it was time for bed even though she hadn't achieved as much as she'd hoped.

The stairs leading to her room seemed steeper tonight. A yawn cracked Jess's mouth wide open as she slipped into the en suite. After shucking her clothes, she stepped beneath the temperamental shower, so tired she didn't care if the water ran hot or cold. All she wanted was to rid her body of the worst of the dust and crawl into the four-poster bed. And dreams. Yeah, she could do with one or two of those.

A mere ten minutes later she slipped beneath the covers, not bothering to don her pajamas. There was no point if she were going to strip off in the middle of the night. Her eyes fluttered closed and she slept.

The dream crept up on her slowly. A touch of fingers trailed across her cheekbone. A kiss on the forehead. A nibble on the side of her neck.

"Hello, sweetheart." His husky voice twisted her insides with yearning. No one had ever called her this way with need throbbing through their words.

Jess smiled. "Hello. I'm glad you're here."

"Brandon," he said, punctuating his name with a lingering kiss on her mouth. His tongue delved between her lips, sweeping her away on the same sensual journey she'd made the previous night. He stroked her tongue with his and explored the recesses of her mouth. A moan of pure delight rumbled deep in her throat. Finally, he lifted his head, cupping her face in his hands and staring deep into her eyes. "What is your name?"

"Jess," she whispered, mesmerized by his gray eyes so light they were almost silver. The heat in those silver eyes made her pulse race with expectation. Soon she would feel the slide of his body against hers, the brush of skin against skin. Eager to touch, she reached up to trace her fingers across his lean cheek, enjoying the friction of rough stubble.

"Jess. I want to love you again." He cocked his head as if waiting for her assent, a lock of black hair falling over his forehead.

Smiling, Jess smoothed the hair away, stilling at the intent expression in his eyes. She lifted the covers and Brandon slipped beneath. His skin was cold, a shiver running down her spine when he pulled her against his large frame. "You need warming."

"Yes," he said, "I do." His hands slid across her shoulders and down her arms until they rested above her elbows. He brushed a line of butterfly kisses across her collarbone and lower until his mouth reached the swells of her breasts. "You are beautiful."

And in her dream she felt like a beautiful swan instead of the tomboy who liked to build things and work with her hands.

Brandon licked down her cleavage as far as he could, palming her breasts in his hands before laving her nipples with the wet rasp of his tongue. Jess sighed her pleasure as his mouth branded her flesh. Her nipples beaded to tight points and she wished he'd take her into his mouth as he had the previous evening. The thought had no sooner formed than his lips fastened around her nipple. Brandon suckled strongly, sending tendrils of pleasure shooting straight to her clit. Immediately it wasn't enough.

"Brandon, stop."

His head jerked up. A dark brow arched. "Stop?"

"I need to touch. I want to see you, explore your body like you explored me last night."

A grin twitched his lips followed by a flash of white teeth. He rolled onto his back, placed his hands behind his head and smiled up at her. "Have at me."

Jess melted to a puddle inside, excited by the opportunity to play the seductress. She pulled the covers off his body feeling the same anticipation she experienced opening presents on Christmas morning. The muscles of his stomach flexed while she looked her fill. Her gaze traveled upward across broad shoulders and an almost hairless chest, across the dark strands of hair, messy and tangled and long enough to brush his collarbone. Slowly, she reached out to test his flesh with her fingers. He was still cold to the touch, but that was a temporary thing. By the time she finished they'd both burn.

She stroked her fingers across a pectoral muscle and he flinched as if he expected something bad to happen. He relaxed quickly, giving her a sexy grin that made her toes curl with lust, her pussy moisten for his possession. Talk about a killer grin. Jess bent her head and raked her tongue across his flat, masculine nipple. Back and forth she licked, his taste reminding her of the outdoors with hints of spicy green. Her breast brushed his chest when she explored further, testing his flesh, nibbling and licking.

"Kiss me," he ordered.

Jess lifted her head to peer at him. "Hey, I'm running the show here, buster. You said I could."

A rough growl vibrated in his chest, silver eyes blazing with heat as he stared up at her. "I did."

Jess grinned. "Well then. Let me do my worst."

Brandon snorted in the way that only a male can, putting loads of expression into the sound. Jess took it to mean he would only take so much taunting. She continued to move down his body, taking her own sweet time, licking his flesh, stroking. His cock swelled against her thigh but she pretended to ignore his erection despite his low, rumbling growls. Tickling his hard abs elicited another canine-like growl. Her fingers moved lower but bypassed his groin to fondle his strong thighs. Jess wedged his thighs apart with her knee and moved into the space she'd made. His legs were long and strong, his feet large—an indicator of cock size so her girlfriends said. Jess measured visually and silently conceded. They weren't wrong.

"How long you gonna torture me?"

"Anyone would think you're complaining," Jess tossed back with a smirk. "This is my dream. I can make up the rules as I go."

"Humph. At least let me touch you."

"Don't think so, but I will move things along. Just for you," she added with a wink in his direction.

"Humph," Brandon snorted again. "That sly wink of yours cancelled everything you said."

"Turn over onto your stomach."

Another low growl sounded. Jess merely grinned and waited for his compliance. With a loud sigh he did and she continued her explorations of his feet. She massaged them lightly until he relaxed. His soles were tough and calloused as though he walked barefoot often. She cupped his ankle in one hand and stroked his lightly furred calf. Slowly, she worked her way back up his body, hands gliding and kneading his buttocks. Lotion. She needed lotion. Jess paused to lean over and open the set of drawers beside her bed. Straining slightly, she plucked a bottle of vanilla lotion from the drawer before sliding it shut again. She flicked the lid open and squeezed a generous dollop into her left palm before setting the bottle aside.

"What are you doing?"

"A surprise. Do you like surprises?"

"No," he said, his husky voice blunt.

"You know for a dream lover you're not very cooperative."
Just my luck. I can't even get things right in my dreams.

"I'm cooperating."

"Humph," Jess snorted. She knew some men were threatened by the fact she was so capable. Things like being able to maintain a vehicle and basic carpentry skills meant she was self-reliant. All the men she'd met and dated had acted okay with her independence at first, but cracks soon appeared when she could outdo them in some of the traditional male roles. Her last boyfriend had told her all she lacked was a penis. His crude suggestion that she purchase a dildo and do everything herself had been the final straw in their relationship.

Shaking herself mentally, Jess warmed the lotion in her hands, savoring the light scent of vanilla that filled the air. She spread it across his broad shoulders with a gliding motion, varying the pressure while enjoying the sensation of silky skin and the underlying muscles. Slowly, she worked her thumbs down either side of his spine then paused to straddle his legs without placing any weight on him.

She squeezed more lotion on her hands and concentrated on his tight buttocks. With vigorous kneading strokes she manipulated his flesh, his soft groan telling her he was enjoying the torture. Good, because so was she. The faint tang of arousal combined with vanilla. Her breasts were pulled tight, a delicious ache building in her body. Jess pulled on his butt cheeks, drawing the soft flesh backward and forward so she manipulated his genital area without directly touching. Drawing an unsteady breath, she continued with her sensual torture until she heard a growl.

A grin formed, replaced by a yelp. Brandon moved without warning, turning onto his back, his silver eyes glittering up at her.

Jess glanced at his groin. His cock jutted out, the head swollen and ready for action. Jess moved again, leaning over him. With a lustful sigh, she took him into her mouth without any further preliminaries. Glancing up at his lean face, she saw he watched her, his eyes so full of heat it was a wonder she didn't burn and smolder.

She smoothed her tongue across the tiny slit at the end, collecting a drop of fluid before sucking greedily and licking. Jess made lots of appreciative noise, some mumbled nonsense, but he seemed to enjoy her ministrations as she moved her hands up and down his shaft.

Brandon tensed, a gruff growl vibrating through his body. He threaded his fingers through her hair, lightly massaging her scalp at the same time. His large frame shook but she continued to lick and lave his sensitive tip. Suddenly he spasmed and semen shot into her mouth. Jess swallowed, the nutty taste bursting upon her taste buds. She slowed her licking and sucking, allowing him to guide her by the pressure of his fingers tangled in her hair until he stilled. After a final swipe of her tongue she let his semi-erect cock fall from her mouth.

"Ah, woman." Brandon reached down and hauled her up his body, making the whole move effortless. He covered Jess, pinning her to the mattress and slammed his mouth down on hers. Raw need filled Jess as she sank into the kiss. Desire stabbed through her pussy and she realized how Brandon filled the gap in her life. She had family and friends who loved her, a new home and business, the pleasure of doing something she enjoyed. A dream lover who wasn't afraid to let her be herself.

"Please," she whispered against his lips. "I need you inside me."

Brandon lowered his head to tease one nipple with his lips. He tweaked the other with his fingers, dragging a moan from deep in her throat. Her nipple popped from his mouth, wet and taut from his attentions. "Don't worry, sweetheart. I need you again, and I'm going to thrust inside you hard."

Jess shivered.

"I'm going to go so deep you'll feel me clear to your toes."

Jess's pussy clenched with longing.

"Yeah, sweetheart. You'll get even wetter for me than you are now." Brandon's hand snaked down between her thighs and teased her labia. His talented fingers stroked down her cleft and skimmed across her clit with a light touch. "Yeah, even wetter than this, sweetheart."

She was so wet the slide of his fingers produced a loud squelch. Jess should have felt embarrassed but instead she moaned, the warmth of his fingers searing her swollen flesh. "Are you just gonna talk about it?"

"Don't you like my dirty talk?" he asked with an air of innocence while his busy fingers strummed across her nub.

"I prefer an action man myself," Jess tossed back, gulping at the spike of sensation that rippled right to her toes. His action was pretty good but she wouldn't want it to go to his head. He was way too independent for a dream creation. Jess frowned, wondering if she should take this as a sign.

"Ask and you shall receive." Brandon's grin warmed her through and seconds later he penetrated, going deep as he'd promised. The throbbing hardness of him filled her to perfection. She sucked in a wildly excited breath, clawing frantically at his back as he withdrew and thrust deep again.

"Oh yes. Like that," she said, releasing a breath on a moan. God, yes. He'd managed the perfect angle. Absolutely perfect. Her heart thundered with each powerful thrust of his body. Jess bit down on his shoulder and felt the corresponding jump of his cock deep in her womb.

His pace increased until her womb tightened and exploded in a series of toe-curling spasms. Jess groaned her pleasure and thanked the gods for sending her a dream lover.

Chapter Three

The next morning Jess yanked at yet another weed then sat back on her heels to wipe her brow. The low drone of a motor sent her gaze darting to the driveway. A visitor? Seconds later the mail van pulled up in front of the manor entrance. Jess rose and went to greet the postie. A middle-aged woman with steel-gray hair climbed from the van. She waved and walked around to the rear of her vehicle to retrieve a large box and several letters.

"You must be Jess Whittlebury," she said. "I'm Lois Marsters, the local postie. I need a signature for the parcel. Guessed you were busy so thought I'd save you a trip into the village." She thrust out her free hand before handing over the parcel and mail.

And she wanted to snoop. Jess smiled, shook her hand then accepted the parcel and bundle of envelopes. "Thanks."

The woman studied the rose beds, freshly painted wishing well and the trimmed lavender bushes with avid curiosity before turning back to Jess. "Big job."

"Yes."

The postie's gaze focused on a spot behind her left shoulder. "Ah, I see you have help."

Huh? Jess whirled around and almost swallowed her tongue. Her dream lover stood by the wishing well, a wide grin on his face. Jess's heart kicked up into a racy beat. Her lover. Real?

The shuffle of feet on the gravel drive reminded Jess they had company and she couldn't blurt out stunned questions or go into hysterics right then. It would be all over the village before she could take the man to task. Jess swallowed. "Um . . .yes," she managed.

The man prowled toward her with the grace of a wild beast. Dressed in faded denims, a sparkling white shirt and boots, Brandon looked good enough to eat. Jess licked her lips. Oh boy. She'd practically devoured him during their last torrid session. But he was real. How? Why? She didn't get it. She fixed him with a steely gaze but instead of appearing chastened, his grin merely widened.

"I'm Brandon, a friend of Jessica's." He picked up the postie's hand and kissed the back of it with the finesse of an eighteenth-century gentleman. Then, as a blush settled in the postie's cheeks, Brandon stepped up beside Jess.

"Pleased to meet you both. I'm glad you're not here on your own. You've heard about the attacks? There was another one not far from the church. Old Mrs. Cooper was struck from behind and had her purse stolen. They left her bleeding on the ground."

"Is she all right?" Jess asked.

"They had to take her to the hospital." The postie scowled. "But she's at home now. You take care."

"I'll be with Jess," Brandon said, slipping his arm around her waist. "I'll make sure no harm befalls her."

Jess's breath eased out with an audible hiss. Until he'd touched her she'd still doubted. There was nothing dreamlike about this male. She could feel him. Smell his delicious masculine scent while his husky voice did something to her nether region she wasn't comfortable thinking about in public. Jess was too astonished for anger, but boy he'd better have explanations. And he could wipe that smirk off his face. Jess pinched him hard on the butt. The wretch barely blinked.

Yep, A-1 supreme, solid male.

Brandon stood with his arm curved around Jess's waist as they watched the postie maneuver her red van under an overhanging oak branch. Elation bubbled in him. The desire to shift to wolf and throw back his head in a celebratory howl clawed at his control.

Jess could see him. The other woman had seen him.

He was no longer a transparent entity drifting aimlessly around his old estate. Somehow a second chance was his for the taking. Brandon didn't know how long this gift would last, but determination to grasp every opportunity pounded him.

"Pleasant woman, but a trifle nosy," he said.

Jess tugged from his grasp and whirled on him. "You have some explaining to do, mister." She punctuated each word with an index finger poked in his chest, her brown eyes flashing with fire.

"Jess, I can explain." Brandon restrained his chuckle, judging from her expression amusement would be ill-advised.

Her brow wrinkled in disbelief. "Do it then. Explain to me why I shouldn't call the local cops and have you thrown into jail."

God's teeth. How did he explain to Jess he was a ghost? And a werewolf, if he wanted preciseness. Somehow he thought Jess would want every detail, but would she believe? He sucked in a hasty breath, taking pleasure in the simple act. A quick glance at her face started nerves dancing, something he, as the lord of the manor, had never suffered before.

"Quit stalling. You entered my bed under false pretenses. I have no idea how you did it." Hot color suffused her cheeks. "I thought I was dreaming."

He noticed she didn't deny she'd enjoyed their lovemaking. "I'm a ghost." Brandon watched the disbelief leap onto Jess's face.

"Pull the other leg. It plays *There's a sucker born every day.*"

He wasn't used to women speaking to him with sarcasm lacing their words. "I am Brandon Lupinus, born in the year 1701—"

"You're wearing jeans!" she said scornfully. "Any idiot knows a male in the eighteenth century wore breeches."

That he could change. Brandon flicked his wrist toward his body, willing them to the garb of his time—black satin breeches, a gray shirt and a darker gray waistcoat with black and silver embroidery to match his eyes. "How's this? Or would you prefer something more formal?" Another flick of his wrist and his clothes changed to full evening regalia complete with hat. Brandon swept off his hat and bowed deeply, starting to enjoy her reaction, complete with rounded eyes and gaping mouth.

"I . . . um . . . a ghost?" Jess backed up a couple of steps.

"Too formal for you?" Brandon flicked his wrist again and willed another change. His clothes faded, leaving nothing but skin.

"Will you quit that?" she snapped, taking a bracing breath.

Brandon watched the rise and fall of her breasts with interest. "I thought you liked me this way."

"I do," she grumbled, squeezing her eyes tightly shut. "You're exploiting my weakness and that's got to stop!"

Brandon arched his brows. "Why?"

She spluttered unintelligible sounds, her mouth opening and closing like a fish on dry ground. "I need coffee."

Jess spun away from temptation and stomped up the path toward the front door of the manor. She resisted the siren urge to glance over her shoulder and ogle the picture of masculine beauty displayed for her viewing pleasure. Not that she needed another look. His image was seared into her brain. Tall. Long, dark hair. Broad shoulders. Muscular. Big co . . . A burst of awareness thrummed to life at the apex of her thighs. Jess sucked in a deep breath, causing her nipples to brush against the cotton of her bra. The sensation sashayed straight to her clit and she gasped. Damn! This wasn't meant to happen.

She yanked the door open, shot inside, then slammed it after her.

"Wait for me." Brandon's head popped through the closed door, a fierce glower on his face. "God's teeth." His shoulders appeared and finally, after a torrid curse, he stood in the vestibule clothed in the jeans and T-shirt again. "That never used to hurt so much. I've gained substance but lost the ability to move freely."

Jess shook her head, bemused by the fact he really was a ghost. And her lover. "But I thought the ghost was a wolf," she said suddenly.

"I am. Brandon Lupinus." Brandon transformed before her eyes into a huge black wolf. He prowled toward her, the nails on his paws clicking on the old tiled floor.

All the better to eat you with, my dear. The words from the fairy tale popped into her mind and she backed up rapidly. The wolf followed, its moist breath burning her leg right through her jeans. Jess found herself trapped in the corner with the coatrack. Brandon the wolf kept coming. He jumped up on his hind feet and balanced with his paws on her shoulders. All she could see were teeth. Big. White. Sharp. Jess swallowed.

"He is a ghost," she muttered. "He can't hurt me."

Brandon's mouth opened wider, revealing even more teeth. A long pink tongue snaked out and slapped her on the cheek. *Tasting . . . ready for dinner.* Fear made Jess's heart stall for an instant. She trembled and closed her eyes, unable to look danger directly in the face for a second longer. But instead of a hungry bite, Jess felt a gentle nibble. Her eyes flew open to see Brandon in his human form grinning down at her. Jess's knees buckled with relief and he hauled her up against his chest.

"I haven't eaten anyone before." He playfully nibbled at her chin. "You're the only woman who's ever tempted me." The grin left his face and the color of his eyes changed to pure silver. "You make me hunger."

The sensual heat in his eyes lured Jess. Oh she hungered too. Suddenly it didn't matter if he were different—a werewolf ghost who haunted her manor. She was different—marching out of step with every man she'd ever met. Jess inhaled deeply, sucking in his spicy scent as she decided to take a leap of faith.

She drew his head down and kissed him. Slowly. Lingering. And with no hidden agenda. This was sex. This was mating, and Jess thought it might even be love.

They finally drew back, both breathing heavily. A teasing glint entered his eyes and Jess grabbed his wrist, reading his mind with ease.

"Oh no you don't! I can't concentrate when you're naked."

"Spoilsport."

"I want to know why you're a ghost."

The humor left his face, showing Jess another side of him. Tough. Determined. Strong. "I was cursed by a witch."

Jess took his hand and led him through to the kitchen. The vestibule was no place for a conversation like this. She pushed him into a chair at the wooden table she'd set up at the far end of the kitchen and went for drinks before changing her mind. This seemed like a brandy or port kind of discussion despite the time of day. Jess removed a decanter of port off the sideboard along with two glasses. She plunked them down in front of Brandon. "Pour."

The scent of robust fruit rose into the air as it sloshed into the two glasses. Brandon replaced the glass stopper and slid a glass in her direction.

"It's not a pretty story." His glance held trepidation and self-loathing.

Jess reached for his free hand and squeezed in silent support. "Tell me."

"I was part of a group. A gang, you'd call it now. We played hard. Drinking. Gambling. Whoring. We were wild and out of control, and no one was willing to stop us because we were the sons of gentry. I think the knowledge of the power

we held over the community made us even more dangerous."
Brandon paused to take a sip of port. He snorted. "Last time I
tried that, the bloody stuff poured out my ears. I don't know
what you've done to me but I like it." He took another sip,
seeming to savor the tart fruitiness as it slid down his throat.

"And?" Jess said, prodding for more.

"The last time we were together there were six of us.
We drank steadily all day. The women we'd arranged to visit
never arrived so my friends needed another distraction. We
went hunting. For women. We mounted our horses and rode
through the village rounding up every young maiden we could
find."

Jess took a rapid sip of her port, not liking the way his
story was heading. Her stomach twisted as she steeled herself
to hear the entire tale.

"At first I thought it was funny, but then I saw how terrified the maidens were and how set my friends were on having
them."

"Rape?" Jess felt sick to her stomach, the port sliding
around uneasily.

"Aye, rape. It was wrong, dammit." Brandon's voice
cracked, and he gulped at his port before speaking again.
"We'd locked them in a stable stall and gone to the adjoining
coaching house for ale and sustenance. I started having second
and third thoughts. Dammit, what we did was wrong. The
women were terrified. I'd had sex with some of them before.
They had been willing, but that didn't make what we were
doing right. I pretended I wasn't feeling well, and once my
friends were settled in drinking, I crept out to the stables and
freed the women. Unbeknown to me, one of my friends suspected and followed. He grabbed one of the women. Elsa."

Brandon's face was pale, his hand wrapped around his glass so tightly it was a wonder the crystal didn't break.

"You tried to help." Jess felt his pain along with lingering horror at the situation he described.

"I didn't do enough. Gerald, the leader of our group, raped Elsa, forcing me to watch." Brandon shuddered. "There was blood. So much blood from her broken nose. A couple of the others took turns before Gerald decided I should be next."

"God, Brandon."

His eyes glinted with emotion and his hand shook. "I refused. Elsa struggled and fought them. By that time the escaped women had alerted the blacksmith. He was armed and shot Gerald in the chest. Elsa was already dead. Strangled. My other friends died that day. Everyone except me. I was shot but only wounded with a bullet through the arm. Elsa's friends told everyone I'd tried to help but the rumors of previous pranks had spread. God's teeth, I wish I'd acted like a man and tried to stop them earlier. They wanted to hang me, but Elsa's mother arrived and said she had a more fitting punishment in mind. She cursed me to wander alone. My father, the last remaining Lupinus, died, and the manor was sold." Brandon forced a carefree smile even though it was obvious he bled inside, that the past haunted him grievously. "I've been a ghost werewolf ever since."

Jess scooted her chair closer to Brandon and placed a comforting hand on his shoulder. "What sort of curse? Surely a curse can be broken?"

"The exact words are branded in my mind. *Walk the ghostly world. Howl at the moon. Alone, Brandon Lupinus, until need forces you to act as a decent man should.*"

"Have you tried doing good deeds?"

Brandon snorted. "I didn't eat you."

"Be serious," Jess said, punching him on the arm. "Good deeds always work in the movies."

"Throughout the years I've tried everything to break the damn curse. Nothing works. You and the woman are the only ones who have seen me since the day of the curse. I can't leave the estate grounds to do good deeds. Whenever I try to leave I get sucked back to the manor house."

"But I've heard a wolf howling out in the woods."

"The woods are part of the estate. If I try to go farther, I end up back here. It's hopeless." Brandon shot to his feet and strode across the tiled floor between the table and the kitchen counters. When he ran out of clear space, he turned and repeated the move in reverse. Jess watched him prowl and tried to concentrate. Difficult given the way those jeans hugged his butt.

"And the werewolf thing?" She might as well know everything while she was asking questions.

"My family name is Lupinus. What else would I be? A pussycat?"

"Put that way, I guess it makes sense," Jess said dryly, eyeing his fierce scowl as he prowled her kitchen. The man was definitely not a pussycat.

"Many werewolf families used to live in the village. Over the years they've all died or left, apart from me."

Jess nodded thoughtfully. This explained the number of local werewolf legends. Her gaze drifted to Brandon. Tavistock Manor might harbor a ghost but the ghost bore his own scars. Jess replayed the agony she'd heard in his voice as he'd recounted his tale. There had to be something they could do to break the curse. Then a traitorous thought crept stealthily into her mind. Her dream lover was real. If the curse remained intact, he would stay with her. Jess stood abruptly. "Enough feeling sorry for yourself. I need to finish the gardens, and since it appears you're no longer ghostly you can help me prepare for the first guests."

Later that night, they sat down to dinner in the kitchen. Or rather, Jess did. Brandon merely sipped a glass of port since he didn't require food.

Her hair was windblown and sticking up at the back. A faint dusty mark marred the tanned smoothness of one cheek. Brandon thought she was beautiful. His cock jerked at the idea of loving her tonight. He hoped she was agreeable. During the years as a ghost he'd lived alone. Spending time with her was a gift.

"What?" she asked, pausing with a forkful of potato halfway to her mouth. Her brown eyes sparkled with silent laughter as if she could read his thoughts.

"Have you come across the plans my father commissioned for the garden and grounds?"

She set her fork down. "There are original plans?"

He nodded. "Probably in—"

A ghostly howl cut through the darkness.

"What the hell?" Brandon leapt to his feet and headed for the front door.

"A relation?" Jess asked, hurrying after him.

"I am the last of my line. The English gray wolf is extinct. That, madam, is someone playing a joke." Brandon faded through the door and strode outside toward the woods. Jess opened the door and ran to keep up with him.

The howl filled the valley again, echoing in a menacing

manner that made his skin crawl. His gut cried danger and Brandon slowed to glance over his shoulder. "Jess, you should stay at the house. It's not safe out here."

"You're out here. Besides, when I catch whoever is out there playing tricks, I'm going to wring their neck."

Brandon stopped and Jess plowed into the back of him. "Jess, please. This doesn't feel right. You heard the postie. A woman was attacked. They could be attempting to lure you out of the house." Caring throbbed in his voice, a giveaway of his growing feelings for her. "Please, if you won't return to the manor, stay here. Behind this oak so you can hide if anyone comes this way."

"What about you?"

"Ah, Jess." His throat tightened at her concern for him, a man who was already dead. This woman was special. Eventually another man would figure that out—a man who was alive and could give her children. He'd have to stand aside then. The witch's curse would take on a whole new level in the torture stakes. "A ghost can't die again." *But they could suffer . . .*

Jess stared at him, sensing the same malevolence in the woods. On most nights the trees rustled, insects chattered and the call of night birds pierced the silence. There were occasional deer, along with sightings of nocturnal badgers. This silence was preternatural. Not a twig or leaf moved. "I'll wait here until I know it's safe."

"Thank you." Brandon pressed a hard kiss to her lips before he shifted smoothly to wolf, faded to a mere shadow and prowled down the winding deer track that cut through the woods.

He'd disappeared before her eyes. Neat trick. Another howl cut through the silence of the wood. Unease shot through her, goose bumps springing to life on her arms and legs. The howl cut off midpoint, leaving pulsing silence. Jess crept from her hiding place, the need to know what was happening a compulsion. With her body poised for flight, Jess checked the path ahead, moving cautiously. The path widened into a clearing. The bubble of water told her this was the clearing with the pool. With clouds obscuring most of the moon, dark, forbidding shadows filled the opening in the trees. Another step gave her a full visual. A vehicle was parked at the far end. The headlights were off but the driver's door was open, giving enough light for Jess to see three men, two seated on the hood of the vehicle while another fiddled with some sort of equipment.

"What's wrong with the sound system? Try it again," one said.

Jess glared at the trio, irritated to see them on her land. But what she couldn't understand was why.

"Must have jammed or somethin'. Why don't the two of you start digging over at the far end of the clearing while I fix this? We need to bury the gear before the cops decide to do a search." His friends picked up a shovel each and one plucked a lantern from inside the vehicle. Once it was lit they wandered away, the bob of the lantern light detailing their progress. Jess scowled, turning back to watch the one remaining. Stolen goods. They were burying stolen goods on her property! The man fiddled with several buttons before the call of a wolf filled the clearing.

Without warning it shut off. The man let out a startled cry of terror.

His friends came running.

"What the fuck?"

"What's goin' on?"

The one who had cried out pointed at something Jess couldn't see. Before she had time to react further, a wolf howl filled the clearing. It was loud. Eerie. Different from the one on the machine. A shiver worked through Jess even though she guessed it was Brandon. The call brought home reality. She was not only living and having sex with a ghost—he was a werewolf as well—a powerful creature capable of inflicting harm. The thought gave her pause until finally a grin crawled across her face. He'd never hurt her, not when he held her with such tenderness. If he'd wanted to hurt her, he'd have done it by now. Jess settled back to watch the show.

Chapter Four

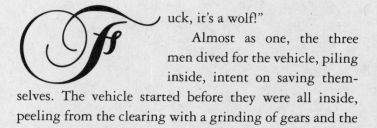uck, it's a wolf!"

Almost as one, the three men dived for the vehicle, piling inside, intent on saving themselves. The vehicle started before they were all inside, peeling from the clearing with a grinding of gears and the screech of tires attempting to grip the grassy surface.

"It bit me!" A pained curse echoed even as the man struggled to jump into the moving vehicle. He clawed his way in while the vehicle fishtailed toward a track Jess hadn't known existed. Since they were preoccupied, Jess stood and openly watched.

The driver calmed and the tires gained enough purchase for him to straighten the vehicle. It sped down the track with Brandon pursuing in his wolf form. Suddenly, he stopped dead. It was as if he'd hit a wall and his howl of surprise told her it was unexpected. The headlights of the vehicle faded and Brandon changed to human form. A flick of his wrist covered his naked limbs with clothes before she had a chance to savor the sight.

"Bother," she muttered.

"Jess, you can come out now."

"Oops."

"I know you're there." Amusement shaded his stern tone, and Jess took heart. It wasn't as if he could put her over his knee and spank her. "Don't tempt me to spank you," he added dryly.

Jess stopped short in shock. She hadn't said that. She hadn't!

Brandon sauntered up to her with a ground-eating stride. He looked strong, vital and pissed. "I told you to wait."

"It's my land, my responsibility," Jess said. "I needed to know what was happening. Besides, I was careful. They never knew I was there. Can you read my mind? And what happened?"

Brandon's brow knit in a deeper frown. "They crossed the manor boundary. I can't. At least I didn't end up at the manor. Odd, but since you arrived the rules keep evolving. No mind reading. Spanking was a safe guess."

"Oh."

"Is that all you have to say? No recriminations for letting them get away?"

A surge of sympathy hit Jess and she reached up to stroke his cheek. "It wasn't your fault. Besides, you put the fear of God into them. They'll think twice before they return. It's a pity they didn't have a chance to bury their loot. Did you hear them?"

"Yeah."

Jess giggled. "It was like watching a cartoon in real life."

Brandon's mouth twitched. "Not so funny for them. You'll report them tomorrow."

"I will," Jess agreed, taking his hand in hers. "Let's go home. I'd like a shower and then bed." She slanted him a come-hither glance. "I'm thinking you should join me. In both places."

"Yes," he said simply, his easy agreement making her heart swell and a familiar low pressure gather between her legs.

They arrived back at the manor in breathless laughter, the return journey even quicker than the outward one.

"Last one in the shower has to scrub the other's back." Brandon disappeared straight through the door, the trick making her blink even though she'd seen it before.

Jess yanked open the door and hurried through. She might arrive in the shower last but she bet she could make him suffer first. To even the odds, she started to undress on the way up the stairs, flinging her clothes over her shoulder and letting them lie where they fell. She heard the shower door in the en suite open and the water start with a sullen hiss. She really needed to get that fixed. Sex in the shower wouldn't be much fun with that pitiful water flow. Jess stooped to remove her boots, jeans and underwear before stepping into the shower with Brandon. The water dripped down his face, splashed over broad, muscular shoulders and ran down his flanks. Jess reached out to touch, following a rivulet of water down his body. Hard to believe he was a ghost.

A hungry look filled his eyes before he took her mouth. With urgency thrumming through her veins, Jess welcomed his invasion. She curled close, his touch sending an intense burst of heat straight to her pussy. Moisture trickled between her legs and instantly she had to get closer, let the fire engulf her.

"Inside me. Now," she pleaded between kisses.

"Yes." Brandon spread her legs and lifted at the same time, opening her body for his possession. His cock probed her entrance while Jess gripped his shoulders tightly. Looking down, she watched him push inside her body.

Slowly—one increment at a time—his cock disappeared. As his penis widened and swelled, he stretched her pussy in a delicious assault.

It was arousing. It was sexy. And it felt damned amazing. Jess bit her bottom lip to stop her moan of pleasure.

Once he was fully seated, Jess wrapped her thighs around his waist and held tight. He remained still inside her for the longest time while fire bloomed and swarmed over her body. Her clit pulsed against his flesh, climax within her grasp already, but she desperately needed to move. She rocked against him, but his greater strength prevented her from moving at the right angle.

"Oh, Brandon. Please move. I need you to move. Please. *Please.*"

"I love making you crazy like this. Your eyes glow. You look beautiful," he whispered before kissing her tenderly.

"I'm not beautiful," she protested.

"You are to me. I have never wanted anyone the way I want you now." Brandon pistoned his hips in a lazy thrust, but it wasn't enough.

Frustrated, Jess dug her nails into his back and bit him lightly on the shoulder in a warning for him to stop teasing. Brandon laughed, a joyous sound that upped the savage ache in her womb. God, she loved this man-werewolf-ghost. It had happened so quickly, but she held not a shred of doubt as to her feelings. Brandon was the one she wanted.

.   .   .

Brandon thrust lazily, loving the weight of her in his arms, the feel of her and the feminine musk that was uniquely hers. Then a truth ripped into his mind. He froze fully seated with her womb clutching at his cock and pulsing seductively.

She loved him.

Joy spread through him. He withdrew and thrust inside her hard. Rapidly. Striking deep, the angle perfect for both of them. Jess's womb tightened an instant before a keening cry escaped her throat. He felt the shivers and spasms that racked her body before he too convulsed with the force of his release.

Slowly he came back. The meager trickle of water from the showerhead had turned cold. Brandon kissed her shoulder before their bodies separated and Jess stood. She grabbed the soap and ran it over her breasts, over her belly and between her legs. When she shivered, Brandon helped her remove the soap and turned off the shower, glad years of observing had helped him keep up with new advances in technology.

They left the shower stall and Jess grabbed a sunshine yellow towel off the wooden towel rack to her right. She ran the towel over her limbs while Brandon thought himself dry and it happened. Fascinated, he watched her pick up a bottle from the vanity unit and smooth lotion smelling of sweet flowers across her skin. Next, she dragged a comb through her short hair, pulling a face at the mirror. She picked up a pink brush and spread tooth powder onto it before cleaning her teeth. Then she turned to him.

"I'm ready for bed. How about you?"

Brandon glanced wryly at his cock. "Yep, ready."

Hand in hand, they left the small room and turned into the master chamber. The covers on the four-poster were rumpled from their morning loving and Jess padded across to the bed to straighten them.

Although her arms, legs and face were tanned, the rest of her skin was the color of rich cream. Brandon smacked his lips, his eyes lingering on the curve of her buttocks. Hungry couldn't begin to describe the way he felt when he gazed at Jess. Being with her filled the emptiness that had assailed him during the long years alone.

His woman.

God, he wanted her so much, wanted to brand and stamp her with his possession and never let her go. But that wasn't fair. She was alive—living and breathing beauty. She deserved a man who could give her a family. Children. Grandchildren. She deserved a man she could grow old with and enjoy both the good and bad things thrown at them by life. A few more days. Just a few more days to store memories to sustain him into the future, then he'd do the right thing and walk away, leaving the way open for another man.

Decision made, he prowled toward her. "Ready for more?"

Jess chuckled, a throaty sound that jerked his cock to attention. "Round two. Bring it on."

Laughing, he scooped her off her feet, tossing her onto the middle of the mattress. The bed protested with a grumpy creak, one of the pulled-back curtains swishing free of its tie. Brandon leapt, and pinning her in the middle of the bed, he proceeded to torment her with sensual precision. He licked her breasts, shaping and molding them in his hands while wedging her thighs apart with his knee.

"I'm going to love you so well you won't walk for a week," he whispered, catching her gaze with his to impart his determination.

Jess's breath came out with a whoosh. "You've remembered I need to finish the redecorating and gardening before the start of summer?"

"Yeah, but I'll help. Two sets of hands will make things go faster." Brandon finally took a nipple deep into his mouth. He loved the hitch in her breathing when he did that so he drew hard before repeating the move with her other breast.

"Does an eighteenth-century male know how to paint and wallpaper?"

"You will show me," he said, grinning with arrogance. His smile slipped a fraction when he thought of never spending time with her again, of watching another man from afar. He swallowed and lowered his head to kiss her, nuzzling and sucking her lips. His tongue swept deep into her mouth, his lovemaking taking on an edge of desperation. Brandon pushed his cock deep into her body, her warmth sending waves of sensation through his cooler body. He continued to kiss and explore her breasts, her mouth, her shoulders and belly until he knew he'd be able to bring her to life in his mind for all time. Then he started to rock deep into her womb, heated by the dripping honey that eased his way. Brandon tasted soap and flowers from her lotion, shaped her curves with his hands, listened to the encouraging moans she made deep in her throat, and whispered of all he was going to do to her during the long night.

She climaxed quickly as they rocked together and Brandon stoked the flames higher, determined to hold back until she came again, clutching his cock so sweetly that he wanted to shift and howl triumphantly at the moon.

The night passed all too quickly. Brandon lost count of the number of times they came but his senses wallowed in the pleasure and he built a catalog of memories to hold next to his heart for when he was alone again.

The days passed in busy preparations for the opening of Tavistock Manor as a bed and breakfast. Gardens were restored to their former splendor and bulbs sprouted, bringing the promise of warmer weather. Brandon and Jess spent time gardening, decorating rooms and exploring the large manor grounds together, trying to decide what she should do with the remaining land.

Jess returned from a quick trip to the village to pick up supplies and mail. She found Brandon stripping wallpaper from the final room on the second floor. "There was another robbery last weekend. Mrs. Robinson, the craft store owner, was attacked while she was walking her dog after dinner. This time they had a gun."

"Was she hurt?" Brandon wished he could help, but he could do nothing confined to the manor grounds.

"They shot her terrier dog. Evidently she's heartbroken."

Brandon removed the last section of wallpaper and turned to Jess. "I don't like the sound of this. What have the authorities done?"

"The police? I heard they've increased the night patrols. And the villagers have started a system where they look out for their neighbors."

"I have no faith in the law. They didn't do anything when you reported the men on your property," Brandon snarled, his expression fierce and scary.

Jess shrugged uneasily. Brandon's moods were up and down and she didn't understand why. "The vehicle was stolen. I wasn't able to give them a good enough description of the men, but I'm confident they'll catch them." She forced a grin. "At least the only wolf who howls around here now is you."

"I'm going to the woods. I need to run."

"I'll give you an hour then come to meet you," Jess said.

Brandon hesitated before nodding. "Be careful." He kissed her in the familiar way that made her toes curl within her boots before striding through the open door, shifting to black wolf as she watched.

Jess smiled. If ever a man made her heart pound, it was Brandon Lupinus. A part of her was selfishly glad he'd been cursed since otherwise she'd never have met him. Her breasts tingled as her mind drifted to sex and how good it was between them. Jess tidied away the strips of discarded paper and started to prepare the room for painting. Another four-poster bed stood in the middle of the room, covered with sheets to keep the worst of the dust off while the room was decorated. The floor was bare wood since the carpet was rolled up. Once she hung new bed and matching window curtains, the room with its own balcony and view over the woods would be popular with guests.

Jess filled the last small hole in the wall nearest the door and set the bowl of filler aside. Time to meet up with Brandon. She took the path that wound through the gardens. It led behind the house and into the woods—a path that circled through the oaks and beech trees and back to the front of the manor. A small brook bubbled busily as it wound its way to join the Mercep River. Jess brushed past a willow tree growing on the banks of the brook and headed deeper into the woods. The afternoon sun shed dappled patterns over the ground. A bee buzzed around the early wildflowers and a thrush twittered cheerfully from the low branches of an oak.

Jess walked slowly, enjoying the fresh air and savoring the peacefulness. Sometimes she had to pinch herself to remember the manor belonged to her. The tomboy was fast becoming a success story.

A short howl pierced the air. Jess smiled, her heart jumping into a crazy beat of excitement. Brandon. Maybe she could entice him into making love outdoors . . .

Chapter Five

randon's head jerked up at the call of the wolf, cut off before it wound into full howl. His hackles rose and a snarl vibrated deep in his chest. He scented for intruders, cocking his ears at the sweaty stink of man. When a woman's scream rippled through the air, Brandon broke into a run. Jess? Fear kicked him in the gut and he upped his pace, cutting through the woods instead of taking the path, heading toward the sound. Blackberry and bracken ripped at his thick coat but Brandon kept going, terrified for Jess's safety. God, he loved her so much. He didn't intend to fail again, especially when it came to Jess. When the clearing came into sight he slowed to take stock, his sides heaving from exertion.

Three men. Two holding a young woman while the third pointed a gun. Not Jess. His nose twitched at the sweet stench of alcohol and something else. Drugs? Worry escalated as he debated how to proceed.

The two men held the woman firmly, squeezing her breasts, fondling her ass and worse. Her sobbing pleas tugged at him. Elsa had cried and pleaded.

"Take your time, boys," the gunman said. "We won't be disturbed here."

One of the men ripped off her shirt. The woman screamed, the sound cut off abruptly when he slapped her face. She sobbed, her thin shoulders shaking. Brandon felt her fear. It shimmered in the air, tearing at his guts, ripping the scabs off memories.

The gunman first. Brandon slithered closer on his belly until he was in position to attack. He leapt, striking the man directly in the chest, teeth snapping as a feral growl rippled from his throat.

The woman cowered, screaming again in panic.

"What the fuck?" one of the men cursed.

Yep, they could see him well enough. As he'd hoped, the gun flew from the man's grasp at the force of his weight. Brandon grabbed the man's leg and hauled him along the rough ground with not the slightest remorse.

"Get him away from me, you morons!"

Brandon sank his teeth in a little farther and the man ceased his fight. Not dead. Fainted.

The other two men released the woman and backed away. Probably heading for their vehicle. Brandon stalked them, cutting off easy escape. He growled.

"Fuck, told you this was a bad idea," one of the men snapped.

Brandon growled low and menacing. He should have spoken up instead of going along. Acted like a man. A leader instead of a blind follower. *As Brandon should have with Elsa.* Fury built in him. He'd make them sorry.

"Brandon! Watch out! He has a gun." Jess's terrified warning pierced his anger.

God's teeth, Jess *was* here. In danger, but he had to save the girl first. He growled fiercely.

The man he'd jumped had regained consciousness and possession of the gun. He aimed it at the girl and squeezed the trigger. Brandon leapt in front of the girl without a second thought. He felt the bullet rip into his shoulder. Impossible. He was a ghost. Yes, he had substance, but he could still fade out enough to pass through solid objects. The scent of blood filled the air. His blood. Brandon faltered. Another shot echoed in the clearing, slamming into his side. Pain hit him but he urged the woman behind a large tree to safety, nudging her with his body. His head swam, a peculiar blackness crawling through his mind. The shifting process started, the bullets popping from his shoulder and side as he changed from wolf to man.

"Brandon?" Jess's panic was clear. She couldn't see him. Brandon stood abruptly, wavering for an instant, desperate to get to Jess. He felt weird. Different. His clothes! His eyes widened as he stared at his black breeches. They were from his time—the clothes he'd worn on the day Elsa died. They were covered with blood—both Elsa's and his.

Walk the ghostly world. Howl at the moon. Alone, Brandon Lupinus, until need forces you to act as a decent man should.

A laugh burst from his tight throat. The curse. It was broken! He had fulfilled the terms of the curse by helping the woman.

He whirled around, elation filling him. Jess. He needed to hold her with human instead of ghostly arms, to kiss her and love her as a man. He ran into the clearing, searching for his love.

Where was she?

A third shot rang out.

"No!" His cry of horror ripped through the clearing. He covered the ground to Jess's side in seconds flat, squatting at her side.

Too late.

Pain filled her eyes and blood bubbled from a hole in her chest. Brandon cradled her in his arms. "Jess, sweetheart. Hold on. I'll get help. Hold on. You can't die. *I love you.*"

"Love you." Her eyes fluttered closed and she went limp in his arms. A ghostly form separated from her body as he watched.

"No!" Brandon checked for a pulse. Nothing. He shook her but she remained still. Tears welled in his eyes, spilling down his cheeks. In the distance, a siren sounded. It moved progressively closer. The girl must have found help from a night patrol. Relief was tinged with pain.

Too late for Jess.

He'd lost her.

Brandon stood and turned to face her murderer, fury rippling through him in a giant red wave.

A fourth shot echoed in the clearing. With astonishment Brandon stepped back, pain clawing at his chest. Fresh blood bloomed on his white shirt and waistcoat. He staggered then fell, his world turning black.

"Brandon, wake up." The scent of flowers and woman dragged him from the dark. Cool, smooth hands wiped his brow and straightened his clothes.

"Jess?" Brandon bolted upright, his head going straight through her arm.

Jess laughed. "Whoa, that was weird! I hope we can still make love."

"You're a ghost." Sorrow throbbed in his heart. He hadn't managed to save Jess. She'd never have children or grow old. "You'll never see your family again unless they visit the manor."

"A ghost?" Jess frowned. "I can't leave?"

"I don't think so."

Her forehead smoothed out. "I guess that will be okay. I love the manor." She stroked his cheek. "Don't be sad. You saved the young woman. Besides, we will always be together now."

Brandon drew her close and kissed her tenderly. It was true. They could never be parted now. He smiled with real happiness. "I love you."

"Gather around," the perky guide said. "Legend says Tavistock Manor is haunted by very special ghosts. A werewolf ghost."

"Don't believe in ghosts," a teenage boy muttered from the back of the group.

"Don't be so sure. At full moon, the howl of a wolf echoes through the night. And sometimes when you walk along a passage there are sudden cold spots."

"Humph," the boy repeated his doubt.

Brandon and Jess watched, their heads poking through the wall to survey the latest batch of tourists.

Brandon sighed. "More unbelievers. I believe it's your turn."

"Okay." Jess popped right through the wall, sauntered up to the teenager and tapped him on the shoulder. "Boo!"

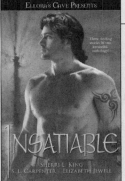
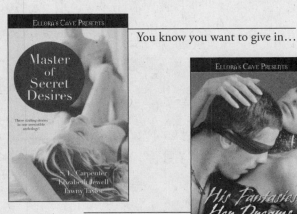